THE MISSING

Bert and Norah

Bernard H. Burgess

Cover designed by Kristy Kennedy-Black, ideacreativeservices.com
Kristy@IdeaCreativeServices.com

Bernard H. Burgess
Visit my website atwww.facebook.com/Coywolf.publishing
Email: Bburg2975@gmail.com

Printed in the United States of America

First Printing: November 2018

Revised: August 2019

Coywolf Publishing

Facebook: The Bert and Norah Mysteries

ISBN-13 978-0-9600069-0-8

DEDICATION

I dedicate this book and story to my daughter, Heidi, with whom circumstances have caused too many of our years together to go missing. In the final analysis of this story, love and belief lead to a greater understanding of things we may not have understood. So it is with the love I have for and the belief I have in the first love of my life, my daughter.

ACKNOWLEDGMENTS

I want to thank all those people who have helped in various ways with my writing and the creation of this book. My wife, Ruth, and her mother, Clara Bass, were the first to read my story in draft form and give me feedback, suggestions, and positive support. Shortly behind them were good friends, Frances Henderson and Tammy Bass. Their support and encouragement have been even more important than their suggestions and grammatical improvements.

Granddaughter, Hailey Marks, of HM Photography, did a fantastic job with a difficult subject and produced a very good author photo for the back cover.

Kristy Kennedy-Black, of ideacreativeservices.com designed a fantastic cover. It is not only eye-catching but captures the essence of the story.

My inspiration to write comes from my father and mother, Bernard and Ruth Burgess; daughter Heidi Myers, my brother David Burgess, and my five grandchildren and great grandchild.

TABLE OF CONTENTS

CHAPTER ONE: THE MYSTERY MAN

Albert Lynnes, Bert, as he was usually known, relaxed and sipped his coffee on the front porch of his Cody, Wyoming, log home, situated west of town in the North Fork valley. It was a beautiful fall morning in October 2017. The reds and yellows of the shrubs and sparse deciduous trees accented the beauty of this North Fork of the Shoshone River. Nestled between the mountains and ridges, the Shoshone River followed this valley as it snaked westward toward the east entrance of the Nation's first national park. President Teddy Roosevelt referred to this drive up the Yellowstone Highway as "the most scenic 52 miles in America."

Just west of Cody, the greys, yellows, and browns of the often-sheer cliff facings plummeted down to enclose three tunnels totaling almost a mile in length. They connected Cody to the Buffalo Bill Dam and Reservoir. This reservoir accented the east end of the North Fork valley like a crown jewel, atop the throne at the west end, Yellowstone National Park.

Bert fit well into this western setting and lifestyle. A retired Army officer, he had always stayed in good shape and worked out regularly. He was only about five feet, eight inches tall, but he had the strength, stamina, and work ethic of men half his age. His dark brown hair was only slightly giving away his age with a little bit of greying around the edges. He was a gun owner, outdoorsman, and hunter, and had always loved the natural world. His skills and interests were well served in his private investigation business, B & N Investigations.

The ringing cell phone interrupted his quiet reflection on nature's beauty and the peacefulness of the surroundings. "May I help you?" Bert asked.

"Is this B & N Investigations?" The man on the line asked.

Bert instantly felt uneasy with this call. "Yes, this is Bert Lynnes of B & N investigations. How may I help you sir?"

"I want to meet with you in town in an hour to discuss a possible case. Can you be at the Irma Hotel then?" The man spoke in a hushed tone.

Bert checked the time on his phone, looked at his coywolf companion and tracking animal, Missy, lying under his cedar coffee table, and answered back, "Yes, I can meet you at the Irma at nine. Let's grab a coffee and sit outside on the east-side porch area. It's usually quiet there this time of year. What's your name, sir?"

"My name isn't important right now, Mr. Lynnes, for reasons that will be obvious later if we decide to work together." There was an air of superiority in the way this mystery man presented himself.

"Okay, sir, but we won't be doing business unless you're willing to be honest and forthcoming after we meet. I want you to know that before you spend your time going to the Irma. I'm willing to hear what your situation is about and we can go from there, if you're okay with that?" Bert wanted to be clear that he wasn't playing this game.

"Fair enough," the voice on the phone replied, "I will see you at the Irma at nine, but I prefer to meet inside toward the back corner if that's okay with you. I don't want to be on the street."

Bert knew he could find this fellow, but wanted to know anyway, "How will I know you sir? What are you wearing?"

"I'm wearing a leather jacket, no tie, and a brown felt hat with the front brim turned down, Outback style." The man hung up without another word.

Bert walked into the house, with Missy on his heels. He knew this guy was some kind of a professional because he mentioned no tie. Most Wyoming men wouldn't even mention wearing or not wearing a tie. He looked toward the kitchen. "A rather strange phone call. I have to meet this guy at the Irma at nine and see what's going on with him. Wouldn't even tell me his name now. Not sure about this one, Sweetheart."

There was no reply, and he didn't expect one after he remembered that Norah, in spirit, was with her mother who was terminally ill in a Minnesota hospital. He had grown accustomed to this relationship with his wife; a joining of their two realities. The trauma of her unexpected and devastating death in September of 2016, had triggered a dormant "gift" in Bert. It awakened an ability to see and communicate with the spirit of his departed loved one. It was a bond formed by undying love. It held the spirit to the living.

He walked out to the garage and instructed Missy to stay home. Her nearly imperceptible limp was the only reminder of her injury five weeks earlier and her rapid recovery. He got into his dark blue Dodge SUV. He had recently started to jokingly refer to it as the doghouse, because he and Missy spent so much time in it. It was only a 15-minute drive to the Irma Hotel, but he preferred to be early and scope out the situation he was getting into on this Wednesday morning, October 4th. He guided his vehicle down to the Yellowstone Highway and would be going east toward Cody.

As he signaled his left turn onto the highway, his eyes fell upon an older man with brown leather jacket, no hat, and greying hair, standing near the stop sign. This fellow stood silently, looking straight at Bert, and then he raised his right hand and slowly waved. As he did so, a Siberian Husky with dark grey and white markings, lying next to him, raised up to sit on its haunches. This canine also looked at Bert, as he proceeded to turn left onto the road toward Cody. Bert returned a quick wave to them as he made the turn.

Bert guided his vehicle into the right-hand lane to allow an overtaking vehicle to pass and then he looked in his rear-view mirror back to the stop sign, now a quarter of a mile behind him. The man and dog were not in view. "Damn, that's unusual," he said aloud to himself. "I've never seen anyone on foot at that intersection before, much less with a dog. That's a beautiful Husky!" He turned his attention back to driving.

The highway turned into Main Street as it entered Cody, passing by the world-renowned Buffalo Bill Historical Center. Visitors from all over the globe could and did spend hours going through the many halls and exhibits. It was a visual and audible celebration of the Wild West days, made famous by William F. Cody, Buffalo Bill as he was popularly known. The firearms exhibit was one of the most extensive in the world. It and the western art and plains Indians exhibits were Bert's favorites.

A few blocks later, he arrived at the Irma Hotel and parked along the street. This hotel was among the city's most recognizable and desired destinations for locals and visitors alike. It was built in 1902, with a couple of later additions, and was considered by Bill Cody to be "just the sweetest hotel that ever was." He named it after his youngest daughter.

Once inside the Irma, Bert exchanged a few pleasantries with the waitress, Mary, a cute woman in her early forties, with whom he'd chatted a few times before. She said she would bring his usual coffee with cream and honey. He was impressed that she remembered how he liked it.

As he walked to the back, his eyes once again scanned the stunningly beautiful Cherrywood bar given to Bill Cody by Queen Victoria. It's reportedly one of the most sought out and photographed features in the town of Cody. Once he'd chosen a table in the back corner, he leaned back and collected his thoughts about how to deal with this mystery man.

Something told Bert to expect him to be fashionably late. It was about ten after nine when the man walked in and came straight to Bert's table. He was a good-looking fella, about six feet tall, trim and well built, dark hair, and roughly in his fifties. He sat down without a word and without removing his hat, as was customary for most ranchers and cowboys. He looked intently at Bert, then Bert stuck his hand out and broke the ice. "Hello, I'm Bert Lynnes."

"Right now, Bert, just call me Sam if you don't mind," the stranger responded in a strong and clear voice as he shook Bert's hand. "I want to talk a bit with you before we go beyond that. He turned to Mary, who had approached the table. "Honey, if you would, please, a coffee with cream. That's all I want right now. Thanks."

Bert knew there was something familiar about this guy, but he couldn't quite place it. He had seen him before, he was sure of it; but where? "So, Sam, what brings you to town; I don't think you're from here?" He noticed that Sam seemed to make eye contact for just a second with another rancher-looking fella sitting in the middle of the dining room.

Once again, Sam seemed to be sizing up Bert as he just sat back and looked at him without saying anything. His silence continued for a few seconds as Mary brought his coffee. He turned his gaze to her, "Thank you, Mary, you're a good waitress. We'll wave you down if we want anything else."

Mary politely thanked him for his compliment and went back to the other customers. She knew they wanted privacy more than food, right now.

Bert sat quietly, similarly sizing up this stranger. He knew this man's appearance was more of a façade than authentic. The guy looked like he could be a ranch foreman, yet Bert knew he was far more than another cattleman. He was hiding his identity, and Bert knew it. He also wondered how Sam knew Mary's name, since he had not heard it since coming into the restaurant and she had no name tag. Was the brief eye contact with that other customer just a mere coincidence?

"Well, Bert," Sam finally asked, "How reliable are you at protecting the identity of your clients and keeping their business with you in confidence?" He looked Bert squarely in the eyes, obviously reading his facial expressions.

Bert didn't hesitate as he returned Sam's eye contact. "That's the way I do business, Sam. I keep case information confidential between myself and the client, unless the client approves otherwise, such as to coordinate with law enforcement personnel. Just let me know how you want your private information protected, and that'll be done. If I take your case, part of my job is to protect your privacy and your interests. That's true as long as your actions aren't criminal, in which case I'll stop working for you immediately. If that rings true, then I'm not your man."

"Fair enough," Sam judged. "If you take this case, Bert, you will work directly for me and nobody else. You must coordinate only with me and nobody else. Before, during, and after, you are not to disclose anything about this case to anyone, law, media, or other, without my approval. Only you and your closest and most trusted business associates are to know anything about this. Only you are to discuss it with only me. Do you have any problem with that?" Sam leaned back and for just a second glanced in the direction of the customer at the middle table.

Bert sensed a twinge of concern, fear, or maybe even panic in Sam, this time. He noticed the brief glance toward the same man a second time. That guy was in the restaurant when Bert came in. Was he there to check Bert out and make sure he was alone, before Sam entered? He leaned forward, rested his arms on the table, and in a quiet, assuring voice, gave his answer. "No, Sam, I don't have a problem with any of that. Now, can you give me some idea of what you're afraid of?"

Sam was taken back a bit by Bert's question, but he recovered his brief lapse of composure quickly. "I didn't say I was afraid of anything, Bert. I am concerned about something, though, very concerned. I had a close friend and confidant check out your business and you, extensively, and he's convinced me that your business may be what I need. There's a very private matter that I need help with and that help needs to be totally confidential, as I described."

"Would your close friend and confidant be the man at the middle table?" Bert asked.

Sam sat upright, "Well, I guess you're a P. I. after all. I thought we were a little slicker than that. Yes, that man is more than a friend; he's my closest friend from college, more like a brother than a friend."

"I assume he knows all about this case if he's your confidant,"

Bert said. "You might as well bring him over and introduce him. As he apparently told you about our waitress, Mary, we might have her bring out three pieces of their peach pie. It's to die for!"

"I wondered if you picked up on my slip with her name. Guess I'm not as good at this as I thought I'd be. Not my usual day job, as you've probably already guessed." He had a slight smile with that confession.

Bert smiled slyly back, "Yeah, I figured you weren't who you appeared to be. I know that I should know you, but I haven't figured it out yet. I assume you're going to confide more in me if we do business together?"

Sam waved for his friend to join them and motioned for Mary to bring some pie to the table. "Bert, this is my best friend, Jim Atkins. He's the only person besides me who knows that I'm here and why. Jim, this is Bert Lynnes of B & N Investigations."

Bert watched this slender man, at least an inch or two taller than Sam, stride over to their table. From his dress, he certainly looked like a Wyoming cowboy. He wore a black felt hat and wore it very well. His blue jeans were pulled over the tops of black, roper-style, boots, and a denim vest fit comfortably over a long sleeve red and black, plaid shirt. His hair was thick and sandy with a business-like cut. His blue eyes sparkled as he extended a hand and gripped Bert's firmly.

Mary arrived with the pie just then and talk was voluntarily suspended for a few minutes while they chowed down on the first bites. Jim put his fork down first. "Well, Bert, I'm glad to meet you. You have a pretty good website and a very impressive record of successful cases and referrals. Did all those people give you permission to reference their cases?"

Bert knew he was still on guard and on defense. "Yes, all the clients referenced gave me permission to generally list their cases, not in detail, on our site. Like many businesses, we thrive or dry up based upon good referrals and word of mouth."

Sam was done with his pie by now. "So, Bert, tell us about your business in more detail. It seems you have a rather unique and atypical private investigation company."

Bert knew they were going to continue holding back until they were comfortable with him. "Yes sir," he admitted. "We consist of three elements, if you will. There's me, a former military officer and now the grunt of the operation, some might also say the owner. Nobody would say I'm the brains."

They all laughed.

"The real brains of this company are in the psychic I work with to provide insights that aren't intuitively obvious. These inputs are not always crystal clear and often it takes a team effort to make sense of them. She chooses to work only in the background and deals only with me; this keeps what she calls the psychic noise to a minimum. The other brains of the outfit are in a female coywolf. She's not only a unique companion animal but also a very reliable tracker. Once she has a scent, she's very good at finding out who owns it."

Jim piped in, "There's a number of speculations floating around about your psychic, Bert. None of your previous clients admit to having met her. Norah, I think they called her? You say she's an integral part of your team?"

"You bet Jim; our team wouldn't be nearly so effective without her. The business of finding the missing requires a lot of insight, intuition, and often just good luck. To keep her mind clear, she likes to work behind the scene."

Sam sat quietly absorbing all he was hearing. They all sat quietly contemplating everything they'd talked about so far. Sam finally opened up. "Bert, it was quite a feat for me to sneak away from my office for a supposed getaway and drive up here to Cody to talk with you. That's a rare luxury for someone in my position. So, let me tell you what this is about. Then you tell me if you think your company can handle it."

"I'm listening, Sam," Bert said. "I can't give you an honest answer until I know what's going on."

Sam went on. "Suppose a good friend, an executive of a major corporation, came to you in confidence and asked you to help him in a difficult personal situation. He confides that his only son has been kidnapped."

"My first question would be to ask if he's involved the law. If not, why not? That's the first thing he should do." Bert was adamant about that.

Sam continued. "Yes, he has involved the law and they're treating it as they do all kidnappings, so far with no results."

"When was the son taken?" Bert wanted to know.

"Four days ago," said Sam. His voice wavered ever so slightly.

"So, why obtain the services of a private investigator?" Bert asked the question they all knew was coming.

Jim noticed that Sam was looking away; he knew it wasn't from being distracted. "Bert, the reason we are considering your company is that the son was abducted during a company event. The manner and timing of his abduction leaves no other conclusion but that someone on the inside helped plan and execute the kidnapping. For all we really know, it might even have been one of the cops or guards or close staff currently giving the appearance of working to find the boy. We don't know who we can trust, so we need someone who is totally outside the company and the law enforcement; someone we can trust to investigate this and report to the company president what he finds out. That's why we came up here to talk with you. The boy is in grave danger. We think the abductors are deadly serious. This is all given in confidence to you, whether you take the case or not. Okay?"

"Gentlemen, I totally understand the gravity of this situation and it will remain in strict confidence. Let me ponder this while I run to the men's room; one too many coffees today." He got up and proceeded into the next room where the bathrooms were. As he passed by the east windows, he noticed the guy from the stop sign earlier, along with his beautiful Husky, standing along the far sidewalk. They seemed to be contemplating where to go. Bert wondered what they were doing here. His curiosity subsided as he disappeared into the men's room.

Sam and Jim remained at the table, with another coffee delivered cheerfully by Mary, as they compared notes about Bert and company.

Once inside the bathroom, Bert pulled out his phone and did a couple of quick google searches while he "drained the lizard," as he loved to laughingly tell Norah. There was a nagging suspicion that he had to check out in the couple of minutes he was away from the two men. Satisfied from both endeavors, he headed back to the dining room.

He sat back down at the table. "Whew, needed that! About to bust a kidney. Well, gentlemen, I've given this some thought, and

I see why your friend wants a second opinion, to use a medical phrase. This will be a difficult case, given so many unanswered questions, but I find it challenging. I think my business is equipped to do as you ask, or rather as your friend asks. We can bring that boy home, but it'll take some effort, and to be honest, some good luck. So many things could go wrong; we must work closely together and be very careful. So, if you want us, B & N Investigations will be at your service."

Sam spoke up with little hesitation, "Bert, Jim and I both have a good feeling about you. We will suggest to our friend that he hire you. Give me a minute to use the bathroom myself and I will give you the answer."

Bert knew there were no other customers or staff within earshot, so he leaned forward and in a subdued voice, tossed Sam a surprise. "Sam, when you come back you might take down the picture of the Governor and take it to the front desk. It hasn't been signed, I noticed. While you're there, go ahead and sign it. When you get back to the table, Governor, let's go somewhere so we can talk about what really happened to your only daughter and how we're going to bring her home."

Wyoming Governor, Samuel Patterson, sat in stunned silence for a few seconds, then slowly pushed his chair back and stood up. He quietly replied, "Well, Mr. Lynnes, I think I'm beginning to see why you're the man I need for this job. The man I'll trust to get my little girl back safely." With tears struggling to roll down his cheeks, he turned abruptly and walked toward the men's room.

Bert and Jim turned to small talk, continuing to get to know each other.

Out on the sidewalk, a middle-aged man with dark but greying hair, wearing a brown leather jacket and matching hiking boots, seemed to look in Bert's direction through the window, then resumed his walk and motioned to his Husky. They disappeared from Bert's view as they passed the large picture window. Bert thought to himself, "I wonder who that guy is? Never seen him around here."

CHAPTER TWO: WHAT HAPPENED?

Bert, Jim Atkins, and Governor Patterson agreed to resume their discussion at the beautiful Cody City Park, on one of the more remote picnic tables. This park served as the heartbeat of Cody, being situated near the middle of town, close to the high school, close to the many and varied downtown establishments, and within walking distance of the Buffalo Bill Historical Center. A pavilion was the site of many concerts throughout the summer months. It was a nice fall day with a relatively mild 58-degree temperature, blue sky, and almost no wind. It was a great day to be outside. Bert offered to go by Burger King and pick up some sandwiches and drinks for them.

When he caught up with the two men at the table, Bert passed out the lunch, and they exchanged small talk about college football as they quickly ate. After Jim had gathered up their trash and tossed it in a nearby trash can, they leaned toward each other and began to softly tell Bert more details about the kidnapping of the Governor's daughter.

Governor Patterson was hosting an Irish singing group at the old Historic Governor's Mansion in Cheyenne last Saturday evening. His wife, Betsy, and only daughter, sixteen-year-old Samantha, or Sammie as they usually called her, were to help host the event. At the last minute, literally as they were walking out the door of the new Governor's Residence, Sammie stepped on a rock at the edge of their driveway and badly sprained her ankle. They knew she was just going to need some ice, followed by wrapping, and time, but she needed to stay off it for a few days. So, with minutes to go before the evening event, the decision was made to leave Sammie at the Governor's Residence.

Sam and Betsy drove the ten minutes across town to the old

Historic Mansion. They knew that Sammie was mature for her age and more than capable of taking care of herself until they returned in two or three hours. Besides that, one of the security staff was assigned to keep an eye on the Governor's Residence that night. He would generally be in the foyer or around on the grounds.

As the Governor began to host the event with his wife, he confided in the head of security about Sammie's absence. The other five security officers were then given the same information. When Sam greeted his best friend, Jim, around the cocktail bar, he asked Jim if he would go check on Sammie in an hour or two, just to make sure she was doing okay. Jim, of course, was more than happy to do that. His wife, Andrea, was fine with staying behind at the event until his return.

The evening proceeded very well. The twelve Irish singers were introduced following cocktails and a tour of the mansion. They then performed five of their most popular songs during the dinner. The one-hour mix-and-mingle session was to conclude the evening.

Toward the end of the dinner, at about the two-hour point of the event, Jim said he would take one of the more junior security guards and go check on Sammie. They would give the guard at the residence a chance to change places with the guard accompanying Jim. That young lad could also meet the Irish group that way. The two men left the event and drove the ten minutes to the Governor's residence.

About twenty minutes after Jim and the guard left to check on her, Jim called Governor Patterson and told him they could not find Sammie at the residence. There were no signs of any issue, they just couldn't find her. The Governor called his daughter's cell phone, but there was no answer. He quickly but discreetly found the chief of security and told him that he and his wife were leaving early. The Governor asked the chief to take over the remaining hospitalities toward the singers and apologize for his unexpected absence. He and Betsy hurried to their staff car and sped toward their home.

At the Governor's Residence, the complete absence of clues was unsettling. The doors were all locked and there were no signs of forced entry. The lone guard, Jeremy, was at the front foyer when Jim and the other guard arrived. Jeremy was not aware that Sammie was missing. Nobody had passed his security location all evening. Likewise, there were no signs of a struggle or any foul play. Sammie still was not answering her cell phone, which she apparently had with her, since it was nowhere to be found in the house. She was gone, without a clue as to where or why.

* * *

At midnight that Saturday, Governor and Mrs. Patterson had milled around nervously in the main Library of the Governor's Mansion. The large oak table was surrounded by the Chief of the Cheyenne Police Department, the Sheriff of Laramie County, the Governor's Chief of Staff, the Head of Security, and Jim Atkins. Jim's wife had gone to their home in Laramie. They had reviewed everything they could determine about Sammie's disappearance.

Governor Patterson recounted for Bert the things they had determined or discovered. It seemed apparent that Sammie had left from the rear door off the kitchen and pantry. That was the only door not frequently observed during that time by the guard at the front of the house, and the one security camera that normally scanned that area behind the mansion was out of order. It had been out of order for two days and was scheduled for replacement on Monday. It was about 40 yards from that door to a chain link fence near the street behind the house. An able-bodied person would have no trouble scaling that fence, but Sammie would need assistance to cross it with her sprained ankle.

"Have you heard from anyone asking for a ransom or other demands?" Bert asked.

"Not at this time. We haven't heard a word about this from anyone." Governor Patterson cleared his throat to hold back his emotions.

"Anything else at this time?" Bert wanted to know.

The Governor shook his head. "No, nothing else. No contact, almost no leads to follow. Because of the nature of the crime, the public has so far not been told of the kidnapping. We have just put out a story that my daughter sprained her ankle and must stay off it. That much is true, even if it isn't the whole story. Right now, we don't want this to become a media circus. Once we know more, we'll have to make this known to the public."

Bert was thoughtful for a minute, and then asked, "What makes you think this was an inside job?"

"It seems unlikely that anyone could have done this without an insider's knowledge. Sammie's accident just happened right before the event Saturday night. To take her from our home during the event, someone had to literally have last second information. Also, there was no forced entry and no signs of a struggle. Either someone had the key to one of the doors, knew where the one guard was or was able to induce Sammie to open a door for them." The Governor's voice was showing a growing anger.

"What are the law enforcement folks thinking about that theory?" Bert wanted to know.

"They acknowledge the possibility of an insider. However, they've interviewed everyone having this information that night, and even did lie detector tests on several. Everyone passed. The others have all volunteered for the test and just haven't been tested yet." The Governor sighed in frustration and leaned back.

"Have they checked their phones for calls?" Bert inquired.

The Governor was quick to answer. "Yes, they collected and checked all our phones, even mine and Jim's, for calls and texts. Nothing stands out as suspicious."

"Who, besides you two and the security guys, knew about the change with Sammie?" Bert asked. "Did anyone else have that information during the time of the event?"

Governor Patterson shifted on the wooden park bench. "The only ones we know about are our two wives. My wife, Betsy, was with me literally the entire night and made only one call, about 30 minutes after the event started, to Sammie to check on her. She was fine at that time."

Jim chimed in, "My wife, Andrea, made two calls to our home for our son. She called our home when she knew about Sammie's injury, to tell him we might be late. He wasn't there at that time, so she left a message. When she heard of Sammie's disappearance, Andrea knew we would go by the Patterson's. Sammie is like a little sister to our son; they have known each other their entire lives and are very close; and she's like a daughter to us. We had planned to go to a movie with Andrew, our son, and she wanted him to know we would be late. So, she called and spoke with him just before we left the event."

"Can you tell me about your son, Andrew, please," asked Bert.

Jim replied without hesitation. "Andrew is just twenty years-old, and a senior at the University of Wyoming. He lived in a fraternity on campus until recently. He just moved off campus a few weeks ago to an apartment. He's close enough to stay at our home, on the outskirts of Laramie, when he wants."

Bert scooted back on the bench, which was becoming uncomfortable. "Did the police check for those disposable phones? Could any one of the potential suspects have had and used a cheap phone like that and then tossed it?"

Both the Governor and Jim were uncomfortable with Bert's question. Governor Sam replied after several nervous seconds. "I can't say for sure if any of our police thought to check for those. I didn't think about that possibility, myself. There are several trash cans available at and outside the historic mansion, so it would have been fairly easy to throw one away."

"By some slim chance, have those trash cans not been emptied yet?" Bert wanted to know.

Jim jumped back into the discussion. "Oh, I'm pretty sure all those are picked up on Mondays. Other weekdays, too, I think. They would already be in the landfill by now. The trash goes straight there the same day it's picked up. There would be two more days of trash on top of that day, by now."

"I think we should make sure that those receptacles are checked anyway, just to be sure. Maybe we'll get lucky and they will still have the trash in them, and we can rule this possibility out." Bert leaned forward on the park table. "Otherwise, gentlemen, we have to accept that it is possible for someone that night to have used one of those phones. You can try a lie detector on this point, and maybe you can tell if somebody is lying about that. As I see it, unless we can rule out this possibility, then everyone becomes a potential accomplice. We all know that someone, somehow, tipped off the kidnappers about Sammie being at home. It seems highly probable that they planned to somehow take your daughter while at the event. They had to have time to react to this last-minute change of plans, so this was probably done in the first 30 minutes that night. Plenty of time after that to get rid of the phone. "

Governor Sam Patterson leaned forward with his head slightly down, contemplating the gravity of what they had just discussed. He asked himself the key question. "Who among our six security members would have betrayed us, and why?" He corrected himself. "Seven security guards. One, Jeremy, was at the house with Sammie. He was in the best position to be the traitor, but he's a very nice young man and seems to take his job very seriously. Hard to believe he's the culprit but can't rule him out."

Jim Atkins was also quietly contemplating the various scenarios. He knew that his friend, Sam, was considering, just as Jim himself was acknowledging it, the remote possibility that his best friend, Jim, or his wife, were the accomplices to Sammie's abduction.

Bert was quietly absorbing the disturbing nuances and options within this case. After a couple of minutes, he broke the silence. "Well, Sirs, I think the first undercover move I need to do is to gain access to the old historic mansion and check all the trash containers. Maybe we'll get lucky. We cannot trust anyone else to do this or know that I'm doing it. However you want to give me access, we need to do this immediately. I must get back home soon, if you're ready to move on this, Sir. I have to pack up my things and get on the road to Cheyenne tonight. It'll be dark before I can get there. Once there, I need to get into that building as soon as humanly possible. Tonight!"

The Governor nodded his agreement. "You bet, Bert; I will be back in Cheyenne a couple of hours before you. When you get there, I'll have the key for you to the old mansion."

"One more question, Governor," Bert added quickly, "Can you trust all the other law enforcement people other than your security team? The Sheriff and the Chief of Police, etcetera?"

Sam pondered that question for a few seconds before answering. "Well, hell, I can't say for sure now that you ask. The Sheriff and Chief of Police were among my invited guests. They would have known early on about Sammie's injury."

Bert sat in silence. This was going to be even tougher than he imagined. "Governor, we need to develop a quick code for us to communicate. I'm not famous, but my previous cases have given my company a degree of notoriety. Someone might recognize me and wonder what I'm doing around Cheyenne, especially since I will have to bring along Missy. How about we refer to me as Cody and conduct business very sparingly on the phone. It's a good idea to have a couple of discreet places we can meet to discuss this case. Would you pick at least two, where you'd be comfortable talking and come up with a simple code name for them, something easy to remember. Whenever we discuss meeting, it will always be one hour earlier than the time we set on the phone. If we say we're going to meet at two; that means one. If anyone is trying to keep tabs on you behind your back, this might make it more difficult. We have to assume that the mole will want to know what you're doing."

Governor Patterson stood up. "Bert, I understand, and I think you're right about those precautions. It seems prudent to assume the worst until we know differently."

"One last question," Bert interjected, "are your wives' phones encrypted."

Jim answered right away. "Well, I know that Andrea's phone isn't encrypted, and I doubt that Betsy's is. Why are you asking? Do you think one of those calls may have been intercepted?"

Before Bert could answer, Sam chimed in. "No, Betsy does not have a secure phone, either. Do you think her first call may have been intercepted and that may have tipped off the kidnappers?"

Bert answered, "Gentlemen, I don't know, but I think we have to admit that this is another possibility. It also could explain why the kidnappers were able to respond and change their plans so quickly."

All three men stood up quietly, their minds racing with so many things to consider. With little more to add and much on their minds that had to be done, the three men shook hands and went in different directions to their respective vehicles.

Bert Lynnes left Cody, heading west on the Yellowstone highway, through the tunnels next to the Buffalo Bill Dam and along the massive reservoir. His mind was racing, and he knew he had to be on his best game. "Norah," he said aloud, "I'm going to need your help on this one. I hope you can return soon from your mother's side."

CHAPTER THREE: THE FIRST HOURS

Bert and Missy rolled into Cheyenne just after eight that evening. He'd called Sam about an hour earlier to advise him of his arrival and the Governor said they were going out for a Chinese food carry-out. He said he could meet Bert in the parking lot, briefly, to discreetly hand over the key to the historic mansion. Bert also asked for a piece of Sammie's clothing or a personal item. Missy needed to learn her scent. It was likely that her nose was going to play a role in getting this girl back to her parents.

Bert observed the Governor's private black Ford pickup at the restaurant parking lot and pulled next to it. He walked over to the driver's door and spoke through the window to Sam Patterson, discreetly took the key and Sammie's hairbrush, and went back to the doghouse. He drove away and toward the historic Governor's Mansion on the south side of the city.

When he parked next to the old Mansion, there were no other people in the immediate area, so he put Missy on a leash, knowing she would appear to just be another dog to most people. They walked briskly to the front door, surveying the area for any trash receptacles that might serve the facility. He saw a container on the right front street corner. They proceeded quickly to it.

"Dam," he said quietly to himself. There was only a clean trash bag in the container, nothing else. "Has all the trash been picked up?"

Bert proceeded into the old Mansion, turning on the lights as he entered. If anyone noticed him, he wanted it to look as natural as possible. With Missy at his left side, following his heel command, they proceeded to methodically survey every room of this historic building. It was beautiful and an architects' delight, but he didn't have time to enjoy it. Right now, he was on a mission. He found at least a dozen trash receptacles around the various rooms, but every one of them had a clean and empty trash bag. Nothing! The trash had been picked up and was undoubtedly buried in the landfill. Any hope of proving the disposable phone theory went to the landfill along with the trash.

He shifted his mental gears from the trash cans to the possible kidnapping plan. None of the present theories made any sense unless the kidnapping was originally planned to take place here. So how would they intend to do it?

Besides the main entry door and foyer, there were three other doors leading from the house. One exited toward the south street from the south side library. A second opened to the fenced back yard from the rear of the mansion. The third was a utility door which led from the kitchen and storage area out the north side to a utility driveway. He noted that a small bathroom was nestled in the back-right corner in the storage area behind the kitchen area, obviously intended for use by the staff.

Bert surveyed the main dining room, seated toward the front of the house and off from the kitchen, separated by a hallway which served all the rooms on this floor of the two-story house. The primary men's and women's bathrooms sat off this hallway to the rear and right of the dining room.

Just to rule out Sammie's recent presence in the mansion, he presented her brush to Missy and ordered her: "Missy, find." He followed her as she performed her methodical check of the entire house, downstairs and upstairs, to no avail. Although she seemed to be interested in a few places, including the main and utility room bathrooms, she did not alert anywhere.

As he rewarded Missy's effort with a small meaty treat, he studied how someone could have planned to abduct Sammie that night, with the event in progress. He was drawn to the utility staff toilet near the utility and supply exit. If she had been lured or somehow directed to use that toilet while the dinner or performance was going on, it did seem possible that she could have been overpowered and forced from the utility room via the supply door into a waiting vehicle just outside. This would require precision planning and timing to pull it off without being noticed. However improbable it seemed; he could see no other more plausible way to abduct her during the event. Could this have been the plan, before her injury required a last second change to take her from her home? It would require a minimum of two people to do this; probably three. At least one or two would need to subdue her in or near the toilet and get her out the door into what probably looked like a delivery vehicle, where a driver was waiting to whisk her away.

Bert reasoned that either the abductors were prepositioned and hidden in the Mansion prior to the event and left with the vehicle when notified of the change in plans. Or, the only other plausible option seemed to be that a perp, apparently one of the security staff, was the mole and part of the abduction team, but he stayed on duty here when the plans changed. Either way, at least two abductors departed and went to the new Governor's residence to conduct the kidnapping there. If the kidnapping was planned to take place during the dinner, it is likely that the kitchen staff would have been so busy with the meal that they would have been oblivious to the activity in the adjoining utility room or on the service driveway.

Satisfied that he had at least a temporarily plausible plan for the abduction from the mansion and an explanation for the rapid response to Sammie's injury change, Bert and Missy closed the old

Mansion. They departed for a motel he had made a reservation with on the way to Cheyenne. It was time to sleep on it.

Before going to bed, Bert was able to contact Norah. "How's your Mom doing?" He asked.

"Her life is very near the end," replied Norah. "She's drifted into a coma, just waiting for the last breath. I'm glad I'm here to help her pass on."

"I'm very sorry about that, Sweetheart; I know how close you are to her. I hope she isn't suffering?"

"No, she's been resting and sleeping comfortably before going into the coma. Thankfully, her last hours are not in pain. Are you on another case?" She was not yet aware of the present situation he was in.

Bert answered her quietly. "Yes, baby, I'm on another case that came up this morning. I would like to ask if you are receiving any signs or signals that may pertain to the case I'm currently working?" He knew she had no knowledge of this case yet. Any signs she had would be untainted by knowledge.

Norah was quiet for several seconds, seemingly in reflection. "Bert, I'm sensing gun shots and feeling death. I am feeling like someone connected to your case is going to die, probably from a bullet. I'm not sure if this is a current or a future vision, and it could be that the victim has already been shot."

"Hmmm," responded Bert, "That's interesting. Do you see anything else, Dear?"

She again answered in a thoughtful manner as if contemplating each word. "Sweetheart, I'm feeling fear, I think it's the fear of a young person, probably a woman. I think she's in danger."

"Thanks, Norah, I wondered if you could maybe sense anything on this case just from knowing I'm working on it." Bert had never asked her for a reading without her knowing anything about a case. He was a little surprised that she sensed anything, much less the feeling that someone might be killed. She did sense that a young woman was likely involved as the victim, because of the fear.

Norah wanted to get back with her mother. "Sweetheart, I need to be here for Mom's passing, so I need to go for now. Maybe we can talk each night and I'll see if the spirits will give me anything for the case there. Good night, my love."

"Good night, love. I'll contact you tomorrow night." Bert turned his attention to Missy, as she rolled onto her side, stretched, yawned, and almost immediately went to sleep in her place under the window of the motel room.

He turned out the light before settling into the motel bed, staring at the dark ceiling. Once again, a profound sense of longing and loneliness overtook him. He missed his wife more than he could put into words. The desire to hold her and hug her was sometimes overpowering, and it recalled memories which were both cherished and painful. What do you do when your most heartfelt desires are right before you but can never again be fulfilled? Tears drifted down his cheeks as he slowly welcomed sleep.

* * *

Thursday morning, October 5th, dawned crisp, chilly, and clear. It was a rather typical fall day for Wyoming. Cheyenne was splendid with the many deciduous trees which lined the city streets, displaying their stunning mix of reds, yellows, and browns. With the light breeze, which is considered a still day in Wyoming, the shimmering leaves made this little cow town turned city glisten like a multi-colored jewel. It was one of those rare communities which blended the old west, cow-town past, with the quiet hustle of the present, and the excitement of those visiting from elsewhere.

Bert called Governor Sam Patterson while still in the room at the little "Mom and Pop Motel," where he and Missy spent the night. "Hello Governor, Cody here. Wondering if you'd like to meet for a coffee or breakfast this morning?"

Governor Patterson instantly recognized the code name they'd agreed upon. "Sure, how about nine-o-clock? I can get away then for an hour or so. There's a little restaurant a mile south of I-80 and just west of I-25 about a quarter mile."

Bert was familiar with that area. "Sounds good, Governor, I'll see you there at that time. I'll go inside and get a table if I get there first."

With Missy walked and loaded in the doghouse, Bert got onto Interstate 25 southbound. He slowed a little as he passed the Cheyenne Frontier Days rodeo arena on his left. No matter how many times he drove by it, the grandeur of this one-hundred-twenty-year-old world-famous rodeo still impressed him. Though never a rodeo performer himself, Bert always enjoyed watching those who were. You could close your eyes at this historic venue and almost hear the announcers rattling off the names of world champion cowboys, such as Earl Thode, Casey Tibbs, Jim Shoulders, Ty Murray, Marvin Garrett, Dean Gorsuch, Dean Oliver, Don Gay, Guy Allen, and dozens of others. Likewise, the famous bucking stock. Bulls, such as Hammer, Blueberry Wine, Bushwhacker, and the legendary Charolais/Brahman cross, Bodacious, once considered to be "the world's most dangerous bull." These, and so many other great performers and talented athletes, had graced the history of Frontier Days. Bert's head spun just trying to wrap his mind around all those years of dust, dirt, sweat, and blood.

After Frontier Days, the missiles guarding the entry to F. E. Warren Air Force Base loomed on his right, decommissioned reminders of the cold war days when these sentinels stood silent guard deep in the silos, which were scattered inconspicuously across the region. They were still visible as he made his way the couple of miles to Interstate 80. At that intersection, he pulled off and got on the west side access road going south. Another mile and he turned to the right toward the small restaurant, which would become their code name: "out west."

It was a quarter till eight when Bert parked toward the far side of the restaurant, to keep his and the Governor's vehicles as much out of the public eye as possible. He gave Missy another short stroll along the grassy south side of the property, put her back in the vehicle, and walked into the establishment. It appeared to be the combination of a restaurant and sports bar.

Inside the dining area, he picked a table along the back wall with the fewest customers, ordered two coffees, and scanned the place. He didn't see anyone who looked or acted suspicious; there weren't many there anyway, thankfully. There were only about ten people in the place, including the couple of waiters and cashier.

A man wearing blue jeans, plain brown western boots, tan shirt, and a large outback style black felt hat, walked in. He looked around until seeing Bert and walked over to his table and sat down. "Hello, Cody," Governor Patterson said quietly. "How're you doing this morning?"

"Damn, Sam, I could set my watch by you today. Here right at eight, just like we arranged." Bert sounded impressed. "I'm glad you remembered our time." In a quieter voice, Bert professed, "I like this little restaurant. How about this becomes our 'west place' meeting location?"

"Good, especially since this is more south than west of town," replied Sam.

They ordered breakfast, fixed their coffees to their taste, and leaned toward each other to talk in a subdued tone. Bert knew the Governor expected him to lead the conversation. "Sam, I didn't find any phones or clues last night at the old Mansion, but I did see one possible way the bad guys may have planned to take Sammie. They might have used the utility room off the kitchen and out the utility exit. Other than that, I didn't come up with anything else of substance. How about you? Anything crossed your plate in the last twelve hours?"

"I don't know," Sam replied, "Maybe. The Police Chief is convinced that the young security guard who was at my home that night, Jeremy Holland, must be involved and is likely the mole. He certainly had access and the means. The only thing that troubles me, though, is motive. I just can't see that he had any real motive to betray his trust. He also volunteered for and passed one of the lie detector tests."

Bert paused to digest that bit of information. "I thought about him right off, too, but he just seemed too vulnerable to suspicion. Why would a young guy in what is probably his dream job risk it all like that?"

"Exactly," Sam retorted, "I've never had anything other than praise for this fellow. He seemed to like us, too, especially Sammie. To be honest, I think he may have been a little enamored with her."

"I'll do some checking and see if I can find out more." Bert said. "Anything else, Sam?"

"One of the guards at the Old Mansion that night is also a possible suspect. While we don't have anything concrete on him, his name is Kevin Murphy, we do know that he is heavily in debt and barely hanging onto his house and wife. Money could be a motive?"

Their food showed up, delivered by a slender, brown-haired waitress looking to be in her forties. After she set their plates in front of them, she stood looking at Sam for a few seconds. Then she asked if he knew how much he looked like the Governor. Maybe an autograph would be in order, she suggested.

Sam didn't look up as he was chopping up his eggs. "Yeah, I hear that a lot, Ma'am. They often say I should've been his brother. It'd be an easier life sitting in that office than riding these darn broncs, I suspect. Doubt that my autograph would get you more than a cup of coffee someplace."

She agreed with that and returned to her other duties. No claim to fame for her today, she thought. Bert smiled and suppressed a chuckle.

Between bites, Bert continued their discussion. "Sam, would the Chief of Police have any reason to place blame on the young guard? Maybe to deflect attention from something or someone else?"

The Governor took another bite of sausage and toast, while he pondered Bert's question. "Well, I don't know but the water cooler talk is that he is quite politically ambitious. Apparently, he's told some people that he'd like to be Governor someday. I'm not sure what I'll do if we don't find Sammie soon. I don't know if I could continue being Governor. Maybe the goal of this abduction is to get me to resign or not run for re-election next year." He looked down at his plate intently for a minute, trying unsuccessfully to hold back tears.

Bert jotted down a few notes before looking up from his last bite of food. "Would anyone else stand to gain if you were to not run for re-election next year?"

The Governor regained his composure and thought about that for a good two minutes. "Well, I don't think for one minute that my good friend, Jim Atkins, would be party to any of this, but he has told me and others that he might take a run at Governor when I'm done. I know he wouldn't stoop to this, though. We've been good friends for over twenty years, his wife and mine are also friends, and his son thinks of my daughter as his little sister."

Bert knew that for the Governor to bring this up the thought obviously crossed his mind. "Sam," he said, "I've had good feelings about Jim, too, so that possibility is so remote as to be basically discounted. We must look at every single possibility if we're going to bring your daughter back home. The fact that you have not received a ransom note or any communication is concerning me, Sam. It's been almost six days since she disappeared, and we have nothing to base a motive on."

"So, where do we go from here, Bert, I mean Cody?" Sam inquired.

Bert gave a low chuckle. "I think my time is best spent now in seeing if I can eliminate any of the potential suspects we've talked about. Maybe I can start narrowing the field, so we can focus more on just a couple; one would be better. By the way, Sam, do you think anyone has been killed during this abduction?"

That caught the Governor by surprise. "Nobody's been killed, or even injured, so far as I know. Why do you ask that, Berrr, Cody?"

"Just call me Bert when it's just the two of us talking, if you want. The code name is mainly for on your phone, in case it's being monitored, or around anyone in your office or staff. Speaking of being monitored, from now on, let's leave our phones in the vehicles, whenever we meet. Our adversary may be savvy enough to monitor us through our phones, even if they're off. To your question, my psychic feels that someone may have died or will die, during this. She doesn't know who or if it's male or female."

The Governor saw the wisdom in those precautions. "All good ideas," he said, "I'm very concerned by your psychic's input, Bert. Since nobody has been injured to our knowledge, then either the death occurred somewhere else in the abduction sequence, if it has already occurred, or it will occur in the future. Your psychic is very reliable, isn't she?"

Bert was reassuring. "Yes, Sam, she's very reliable and her visions are always credible. I can't ignore them. I'm concerned by that. Sammie is most valuable to any kidnapper while she's alive, so I think we can assume that she's being held somewhere alive. Our challenge is to figure out who's behind this, so we can determine where they might be holding her. One other possibility exists too, Sam. Could some other person have been watching your residence that night as you were leaving to go to the Historic Mansion? They would've seen your daughter get injured and stay behind, wouldn't they?"

Sam thought about that as he mopped his plate with his last bit of toast. "I suppose that's possible, Bert." He let out a long sigh. "If that's the case, then our suspect list just increased exponentially, didn't it?"

Bert nodded in agreement. "Yeah, I'm afraid so. When you get home today, how about standing on your driveway, where your daughter was injured and returned to the house and look around. See if you can see any likely places where you might have been under surveillance by someone. Maybe we can rule that out? I'll browse by and do the same. In any case, it's highly likely that there were accomplices at the Old Mansion that night."

With Sam's nod of agreement, they settled the bill and departed the sports bar and grill. Bert sat in his vehicle with Missy, watching as the Governor pulled away and headed north toward his office. He spoke to Missy as if she understood. "Girl, so what we have to do is find which one, of at least four suspects, is the bad guy. And, find out if there's another we don't currently suspect. No problem, huh?"

Missy whined and nuzzled his neck and cheek, yawned, and lay back down. "Not her job, I guess?" Bert chuckled to himself. He reached back and stroked her head and neck, feeling her warmth and life. For several minutes, he closed his eyes and sought to connect with Missy's soul, even as he felt his heart reach out to the soul of another. With an increasingly heavy heart, he pulled out of the west place parking lot and headed back toward Cheyenne.

CHAPTER FOUR: WHERE TO BEGIN

Bert was lost in thought as he drove back into Cheyenne. He turned down the street toward the residence of Governor Samuel Patterson, where his daughter was taken last Saturday. When the residence was clearly in view, he pulled over and studied the place.

The Governor's driveway could only be possibly observed from a side street to the east and the street in front to the south. Another mansion to the west would have blocked any view from that direction. The six-foot tall chain link fence, lined inside with thick shrubbery and numerous trees, would make it very difficult to see the driveway from the east. It appeared that only a vehicle sitting on the street in front of the driveway to the south would have had any real chance of seeing Sammie's accident that night.

With this initial impression guiding his continued assessment, Bert resumed his drive along the front of the Governor's house, observing the driveway up to the house from those two or three spots along the far side of the street almost directly in front. Other than that, he had no real view of the front of the house and upper driveway along the rest of the south street. As he turned north on the eastern street, he saw no break in the vegetation which would allow one to see the activity at the front of the house. He concluded that any observer that night seeing Sammie sprain her ankle would have had to be in front of the Governor's home. That individual would have had to be in a car, on foot, or perhaps hidden in the heavy shrubbery near the adjoining house on that side of the street. Perhaps the Governor could shed some light on the first two possibilities?

Comfortable with this evaluation of the observer option, Bert pulled away from the Governor's neighborhood. He didn't want anyone in the area to become suspicious of his vehicle. The less attention he had right now, the better. As he headed back onto Interstate 25, he became aware of Missy's increasing restlessness. He knew she needed a break and a chance to run around. He needed some time to think about how best to proceed with this case. Then he also felt the urge to talk with Norah and see if she had any more impressions or visions about this matter. A perfect place to get away was the Vedauwoo Park.

He piloted his vehicle to Interstate 80, and then headed west toward Laramie. After about 30 minutes, he pulled off the road onto the Vedauwoo Glen Road, going north. The high mountaintop plateau provided views both locally and toward the distant mountain vistas. Only a few scattered trees dotted this open high-country park, which was split by I-80 and extended to the north and south of the interstate. They exited the vehicle near one of the campground picnic tables. It was a chilly day in early October and there were no other visitors at this time, so Bert gave Missy a hug around her chest and neck, burying his face in her soft hair for just a second. Breathing in her life. Then he released her and allowed her to run around on her own volition.

For about thirty minutes, they both investigated several of the strange rock formations for which the area was known. This was one of his favorite spots along this part of southern Wyoming. Along with the sensations from the many, often eerie, rock groupings, he enjoyed the glimpses of the Medicine Bow-Routt National Forest, better known locally as the Snowy Mountains. This heavily forested region to the southwest of Laramie, butted up to the border with Colorado. To a nature lover like Bert, awesome beauty surrounded them in every direction.

Missy loved every second she was out of the vehicle, too. She ran around the various formations, yapping excitedly, pausing only to sniff out an area of interest under a rock or sagebrush.

She uprooted a rodent from under a rock and it barely escaped her sharp teeth as it dove under another nearby stone. She lost interest quickly and resumed her investigation of the thousand other exciting places around her. Bert couldn't help but chuckle with both amusement and a sense of satisfaction as he watched her antics. It was good to give her a break from the car and watch her having fun.

"Time to get to work," he said aloud to himself. The main reason he drove to this solitary place was to be able to think. He knew the chilly Wyoming day would make it very unlikely for other visitors to interrupt his introspections. A light breeze was blowing at this higher elevation, causing him to hike up the collar of his jacket as he sat down at a picnic table with tablet in hand. First, he had to refine a plan for approaching this case.

It seemed to Bert that there were several approaches. For one, he could choose the one most likely suspect and investigate until they could be ruled out, if they could be ruled out. This choice might allow him to zero right in on the accomplice without wasting time on lesser individuals. A second option would be to investigate the least likely of the current suspects, rule them out and then work up to the next least likely, and so forth. This choice could result in narrowing the field quickly to the most suspicious characters. He would then concentrate on those remaining. He wasn't certain enough of any one suspect to be content with either of those options.

So, a compromise choice might be to focus about half his effort on the one suspect who seemed the most suspicious, and about half his time on the others. This would let him keep his attention on the most likely, without taking his eyes off the others, until he could be certain of someone. Given the breadth of suspicious individuals, he liked this blended investigation the best. It seemed like a good way to start, at least. Now, who were the most likely suspects and accomplices to this kidnapping?

Bert quickly concluded that the young security guard, Jeremy Holland, was indeed the most suspect of the bunch. He had to agree with Police Chief Holcomb about that. Holland was at the Governor's house through the entire evening. He knew right away of the daughter's injury and that she was staying home. He was at the mansion throughout the kidnapping, even though he claimed to be at the front foyer and entrance most of the time and didn't see or hear anything suspicious. He was in the perfect position to call his accomplices about the change in plans for Sammie. He was the perfect suspect; maybe too perfect?

The next most likely scenario, he thought, was for an unknown person to be positioned near the driveway entrance onto the street. Anyone in that position would have known immediately of the change in plans for Sammie and was in a perfect position to call that to his crew. The only problem with this concept was exposure. The spy would have been directly in front of the Governor's vehicle as it drove down and exited the driveway onto the street. That is, unless the spy was hidden in the neighboring house's shrubbery. If that was the case, it would have been a ballsy move, because of the daylight hour; however, it was possible. Or, could the perps have planted a camera near the driveway, with a remote monitor?

"Moving right along," Bert said to himself, he began making notes about the next possibility. "As I see it, there almost had to be a rat in the woodpile at the Old Mansion that night," he spoke to the nearest Vedauwoo rock formation. "How else were they going to pull off plan A and kidnap Sammie at the Old Mansion? Had to have an inside rat, I think."

The rocks gave no indication of agreement, continuing to sit in stone cold silence.

"I take from your silence that you don't disagree, at least," he chuckled. Missy had returned, and she also sat looking at him, her sharp nose and eyes giving no hint of her thoughts on the matter. "Hell, you're no help on this, either," he spoke to her. She stood up, yawned, squatted a few feet away to relieve herself, and then trotted off to check out another set of stones. "Wow, is that your answer, then?" He laughed.

Bert came back from his mental break to ponder his own question. For a plan A kidnapping to have taken place at the Old Mansion that night, it seemed almost certain that someone had to be planted inside to ensure success. However, that delivery van might have been the trump card which could possibly have precluded the need for an insider. Maybe?

One possible suspect seemed to be 40-year old Kevin Murphy. He was one of the senior security guards at the Old Mansion. The Governor mentioned him as one the cops were suspicious of. On the surface, Murphy seemed to be an unlikely candidate for treason. He'd been on the police force all his working life and on the Governor's security staff for the past seven years. His record was reportedly impeccable. His loyalty had never been questioned before. However, he evidently had fallen on some hard times financially and was reported to be heavily in debt from his known gambling habit. He was apparently on the edge to the point that his marriage was on the rocks as well. Was he under enough strain to become a Judas and be involved in kidnapping for ransom?

"Then there's the Chief of Police," he thought, "A man apparently driven by ambition. Ambition which includes a possible desire to be governor? Was there enough ambition to create a vacancy by kidnapping the Governor's daughter?" Bert wondered. "He was inside the Historic Mansion the night of the kidnapping, and he was among the first to know about Sammie's injury and staying home. The Chief certainly could be the rat. He dealt with many of the low-life's and thugs, guys who would do anything for a buck, including kidnapping and murder."

"How do I go about investigating a chief of police?" Bert said aloud. The rocks still didn't answer. Missy had returned and was lying under the table. She raised her head, perked her ears forward, then laid her head back down on her legs and closed her eyes. She evidently didn't know, either.

Even the Governor's best friend might be a suspect. Jim Atkins had known Samuel Patterson since they were in college together, twenty-some years and counting. Jim was two years younger than Sam and was the underclassman buddy to an up and coming star, a man destined to become Governor of Wyoming. Jealousy might be a factor. So also, might be ambition. Jim had apparently made it known, even to his best friend, that he might run for Governor if Sam was not in the race. Jim had built a very successful company marketing mining materials around the globe and was very influential in the extensive Wyoming coal industry. He was well known and well connected, politically, being best bud to the Governor. This could position him very well for a run at the Statehouse. The only thing in his way was best friend, Sam. Would he betray his best friend just to get a chance at Governor four years early? Bert's logic said no, but his common sense said maybe.

He then considered the other options, generally considered to be very long shots. The Sheriff, Buster Zimmerman, was a guest for the Old Mansion event; so was the city mayor, Tommy Tomlinson. They were there, they had the means, but was there any motive? So far, at least, Governor Sam didn't think so. "Can I overlook them, and take that chance?" Bert wondered aloud. "And there were about a dozen other invited guests, mostly a couple of military and other regular citizens." Because the absence of the Governor's daughter was not announced to the attendees, none of them appeared to be serious suspects. They couldn't have known. "Or could they?" A little perplexed, Bert looked at Missy, again checking out a few stones she'd missed earlier.

"Can't forget the other five security guards who were there last Saturday," he thought. "Just because the Chief and Sheriff gave them lie detector tests and they passed, and though the law doesn't believe they were involved, there's no guarantee of that." For now, he decided to put them on the back burner and not consider them as likely suspects. Time could change that.

Bert leaned back against the wooden bench, clasped his hands on his stomach, stretched his legs out and rested them on the cross support of the table. He relished the chilly wind going inside his jacket front. Again, he thought out loud. "So, powers-that-be, help me out here. I have at least four possible suspects to keep my eyes on, maybe more I don't know about. I'm going to focus first on the young guard, Jeremy, who seems to be the consensus choice for snake-in-the-grass. There are compelling reasons to consider several others as well and I need to do those secondarily, but simultaneously. It's entirely possible that Jeremy could be just a convenient fall guy for the real Judas."

After pondering the situation for several minutes, Bert decided he needed to contact Norah again and get her psychic input. He would do this when he and Missy got back to the motel. With a whistle, he summoned Missy to the doghouse, closed the lift gate after she hopped inside, and steered his way down the trail toward the entrance back onto Interstate 80. He hesitated as another westbound pickup took the exit to the Vedauwoo Glen Road and stopped to let Bert pass. As Bert turned left to get back onto the interstate toward Cheyenne, he noticed that the truck was still sitting in the same position on the far side of the interstate. Something caught his attention, though. A middle-aged white man was now standing behind the truck. Near and behind was a dog, something like a Siberian Husky, maybe. The man seemed to be watching Bert's vehicle as he sped onto the eastbound lanes and toward the capitol of Wyoming. In a few seconds, as he topped the first knoll, they disappeared from view.

"What's going on?" he said to himself and Missy. "Is this guy keeping me under surveillance? If so, why, and who the hell is he working for?"

CHAPTER FIVE: THE SECURITY CONSULTANT

Bert drove himself and Missy back into Cheyenne, as he continued to formulate his plan into action. It was about three in the afternoon now, and he knew he didn't have much time. The priority, as he saw it, was to determine if the young security guard, Jeremy, was a viable suspect for this crime, and to keep an eye on the other guards who were at the Old Mansion that night.

Missy was an asset most of the time, but especially at times like this. He parked a couple blocks from the Capitol, pulled a military style cap and light military camouflage jacket from his duffel bag. Both he had worn when on active duty. He added a dark mustache from his disguise kit and topped that off with a pair of wire rimmed and lightly yellow tinted glasses. The glasses would hide his eyes just enough to disguise his eye color, without losing eye contact. Satisfied with his look, he patted Missy on her head, placed her on the leash, and together they headed for the state capitol of Wyoming.

As man and animal strolled around the Capitol grounds, it didn't take long to spot a security guard making his rounds. Bert calmly maneuvered Missy toward the guard's path, until their paths crossed. "Typical nice October day for Wyoming, isn't it?" Bert offered as the guard strode up to them.

The guard responded easily, his eyes on Missy. "Yeah, this is just a typical chilly day for this time of year. What on earth are you doing here with an animal like that? A coyote, no less?"

"Well, you're close." Bert replied. "She's a coyote-wolf hybrid, often called a coywolf. They're becoming common in the northeastern US and moving toward this part of the country.

She's not only my companion animal, but she's a working animal as well, helping me track small game and the like."

"What brings you out this way?" the guard asked. "Looks like you served in the Army at one time. So did I, retired from fling-wings out of Fort Rucker."

"Third ID, for me; Rangers," answered Bert, "My hats off to you helicopter drivers! You guys are a God-send for a man who's lost or downed."

The Guard was warming up to a fellow soldier. "What brings you out this way, brother? I get the feeling you're not from these parts."

Bert now had to pretext this man, as distasteful as he found it sometimes. He didn't like being less than candid with anyone, especially a fellow soldier. However, this was one of those cases where it was not only a legal investigation tool, but the only wise thing to do. "I'm from up around Cody, outside of town a ways; I'm doing some security consulting for a couple of big businesses in the Cheyenne area for a few days, maybe a week or two. Just depends."

"Oh man, that's nice, I thought about doing that. That was before I fell into this cushy job." The guard laughed. "Who are you working with around here?"

"I wish I could tell you, my friend, but security means zipped lips, if you know what I mean?" Bert knew this man would understand that and not press him anymore for such details. "Suffice it to say, they're major players in this area and the state. Say Sergeant, while I'm in town, I'd like to find some like-minded guys to have a drink with now and then, when duty allows. Any chance of meeting up with you guys for a beer? I'm on a loose rein tonight, so could join you in a local hangout. If not tonight, then another time maybe? My name's Cody, a nickname really, Cody Winslow. What's yours?"

"Hi, Cody, glad to make your acquaintance. I'm Doug Blanchard, Sergeant Blanchard to the ill-informed." He laughed. "Sure, a lot of us like to hang over at the Outlaw Saloon for an hour or two after work sometimes. We generally grab a table about 5:30 or 6:00 and tell stories and watch the ladies dance. It's a neat place if you aren't too picky. We'll be meeting there tonight. Feel free to join us."

"I think I may just do that, Doug, thanks for the invitation. It'll be nice to talk among friends while I'm out here away from home. I don't suppose I can bring my canine coyote buddy in, her name's Missy, so I won't be able to stay too long." Bert knew he needed an exit strategy. "Speaking of Missy, I probably need to get her back to the motel and feed her. She's tired of field mice." He chuckled. "So, I'll see you after bit at the Outlaw Saloon. Thanks again."

With that, and a nod, both men resumed their previous walks, Bert directing his back in the direction of the doghouse, parked a few blocks away. Missy followed obediently at his left side, in her best heel position. He was always amazed at how well she had learned these basic commands and how reliably she obeyed them. She really was an amazing animal! She was a great conversation starter, too!

* * *

Bert had fed, watered, and walked Missy by 5:50, when he entered the Outlaw Saloon and quickly located the security guards' table. After introducing himself to the four men, including Sergeant Doug Blanchard, Bert, using his alias of Cody, sat down across from Doug and between a middle-aged, seasoned-looking, fellow named Jake. Next to him was a young, thirty-something man called Bud. The fourth, Larry, pulled up an extra chair near Doug. He was another experienced guy who looked as if he was former military. They took an informal vote on the beer, and then ordered a pitcher.

The talk drifted quickly to the upcoming football game between the University of Wyoming Cowboys and the Colorado State Rams. Bert was glad that he had always loved and watched college football, even played a couple years as a linebacker for a junior college in Casper. He had no trouble getting involved in the cussing and discussing of the teams and upcoming game. This was one of those years when the Cowboys had a good team and sported a one-loss record to this point, that against a very good UCLA team early in the season. From football, the conversation migrated to politics, which Bert knew could give him the chance to steer the direction a bit.

"I'm always interested in the who's who of state politics," he told his new friends. "You guys all get to rub elbows with the big boys and make connections. Who's the next unknown to take a run for governor?"

Doug, Jake, and Larry all laughed at almost the exact same time. Jake spoke up. "Well, Cody, us minions don't get the exposure that the big shots do, so I can't think of any of our group about to launch a campaign."

Larry picked up the thought. "One of the law enforcement big shots may throw his hat in the ring, if the rumors are true."

Doug chimed in. "Yeah, that's no joke; or at least not an intentional joke!" They all laughed at that. "Our chief cop is heavily rumored to want to be governor."

"Is that Chief Holcomb?" asked Bert. "Chief of Police? He's considering a run for the Statehouse?"

Doug somewhat snickered. "Yeah, that's what the scuttlebutt says, and no real reason to not believe it. Holcomb is one of those guys who never misses an opportunity to get in the limelight, rub elbows, or suck up to some politician. He'd suck as Governor; nothing like the current one."

Bert picked up that theme. "So, I take it the guys must like Governor Patterson?"

"You bet," replied Doug, "Patterson's an okay, stand-up guy. We'd hate it if he doesn't run for a second term."

This was another opportunity for Bert to explore. "I thought Patterson was a given for another four years. Are you aware of something different?"

Bert noticed the four men all glance at each other, as if hesitant to say anything more. After a few seconds, Larry broke the silence. "Well, we have reason to fear that the Governor may not run for a second term. Something to do with a family matter."

"Oh, really?" Bert exclaimed. "I've heard nothing about that. Has something happened recently that hasn't been made public?"

"Yeah, Cody, there's been a development that we can't talk about, but it has the potential to make Patterson reconsider whether to run for a second term."

"Oh man, that would be awful! I really like Patterson, too. I hope it has nothing to do with any of you guys. I know that security is often among the first to take a hit when the crap hits the fan." Bert hoped this would draw out more discussion.

He was right. The younger man, Bud, interjected his thoughts. "You're right about us taking the hit first. One of my best friends is totally on the chopping block over this. He's divorced with one kid and will probably lose his job and may be lucky if he doesn't go to jail."

"I'm sorry to hear that, Bud," Bert was sympathetic. "However, I don't want to be contrary, but I've been around enough to know that things aren't always as they seem. Is there any chance that your friend might be guilty of what he's accused of?"

All four of the men answered almost simultaneously. Doug came across as the spokesman, though. "Oh, hell no!" he said. "If you knew Jeremy, you'd know that he is totally incapable of doing what they think he did. He's a nice young guy, just naïve. He takes his job more seriously than anyone I know, and he thinks he's got the best job on earth. He loves Patterson and his family. I think he's got a crush on the man's daughter. He's also a died-in-the-wool college football fan, to his detriment. His big mistake is that he got too interested in a game on a critical night and wasn't keeping an eye on his post very well. For that, he may end up in prison. That'd be a damn shame!"

"Wow! That would be a shame," said Bert. "I know we have to expect consequences for getting distracted in this business, and we might get canned. We shouldn't go to prison except under very exceptional circumstances. Must be something serious, apparently? Will probably be on the news soon, I'm guessing. Do you think one of the other coworkers may have set this young man up, maybe out of jealousy or something like that?"

"Well, that's a $24,000 question, and we don't know the answer," confided Jake. One of our guys has some serious money problems and may go bankrupt, among other things. Some guys think he's letting Jeremy take the fall for his deceit."

"Damn, guys, that all really sucks!" Bert interjected. "I hope this lad, Jeremy I think you said his name is, doesn't take the fall for something he didn't do. I hope someone's keeping an eye on the other guy to make sure he isn't taking advantage of a younger guy."

Doug spoke up quickly. "You bet, Cody, I drew that straw. I'm keeping close tabs on this fella; his name is Kevin. He seems to be a decent and honorable guy, but we want to make sure of that and not let Jeremy get the shaft. I'm monitoring his activities, who he associates with, and so on. There is one other concern we have, though, besides Kevin."

"Let me guess," said Bert, "Your Chief of Police?"

Doug was impressed. "You catch on quick, brother, you're right about that. Our Chief is a man driven by political obsession. He wants to be Governor, US Senator, and maybe even POTUS, someday. We have some concern that he might be willing to pin this thing on Jeremy, just to get it moving along. Hell, who knows? He might even be after the kid to take the blame off himself. I wouldn't put it past the egomaniacal bastard."

Bert laughed at that. "I take it you guys aren't too fond of your wonderful Police Chief. Just kinda picked up on that. Hey, guys, I've really enjoyed the chance to hang out with you and talk about mutual interests; been fun. Got to go now, though. I must keep Missy fed and watered, and I need to contact someone tonight, too. I'd like to get together here now and then if that's okay with all of you?"

All four of the men nodded their agreement almost in unison and voiced their enjoyment of Cody's company. He was one of the guys! With that, Bert shook everyone's hand, said good-bye, and headed out to his vehicle and Missy.

As he started the doghouse, he then checked the time, 7:30, 19:30 to military types. He greeted Missy warmly and let out a sigh of relief. "Good meeting in there, Missy girl. Thanks for being patient with me. I think I picked up some valuable insight, at the very least. We might have moved a little bit closer to finding the bad guys." He was sure there were more than one involved. He eased the car out of the crowded parking lot and back toward their motel.

* * *

"Hi, my Sweetheart," he said to Norah, as he leaned back on the motel room chair. He was really glad to see and communicate with her, again. Missy had moved to the cool floor of the bathroom, apparently to get away from the chatter. She was fed, watered, and had a good walk. She even caught a field mouse, one a little too slow for its own good. "How's Mom doing today?"

"She's still in a coma, Honey," Norah said softly. "I'm just staying close by to be there when she transitions. The end to this life appears to be very near, Darling. The next begins soon. I'm worried about the rest of the family. My sister, especially, isn't handling this very well; breaks down several times a day."

"I'm so sorry, Honey," Bert replied. "I know this isn't easy for you, and I probably should be out there for you rather than here."

She didn't wait. "No, Bert, you couldn't do anything if you were there, nobody can. Only time will take care of all of this. I have the feeling that you're needed where you are, and several people are depending on you."

"Well, babe, you're right about that, I think," he admitted, "I was wondering if you're picking up anything about this case? I know I haven't told you anything about it, purposely, just to see what kind of messages may come to you. I'll bring you up to date on the full case, when you feel you have the time."

Norah closed her eyes and looked internally for a good while, before answering him. "Bert, I sense that this is a dangerous case. And something bothers me, Dear. I'm seeing a vision of a fox pursuing a cottontail rabbit. As the fox gets closer the rabbit panics and ducks into a thicket. The fox goes in after it and they disappear for a minute. Then the fox runs out of the thicket at full speed, frightened. A big wolf leaps over the thicket in hot pursuit of the fox. The fox runs for its life and they disappear over the hill. Sweetheart, this is telling me that you, the fox, may be the hunter now, but you are going to become the hunted at some point, by a big adversary. Be very careful, Honey; you're treading on dangerous ground in this case."

He sat quietly for a minute, absorbing her warning. A chill slowly crept up the back of his neck, and he shivered slightly. Norah didn't make such warnings without good reason. "Thank you, my Dear. I'll heed your words and be cautious. I'll keep Missy close, too. She has a sixth sense about these things. Anything else, babe?"

She again paused, and then replied. "I get the same feeling of death, Honey. There'll be death with this case, maybe already, maybe more. I have no idea what this last thing means, Sweetheart, but the number 104 just passed through my mind. These numbers usually mean something significant, but they aren't always revealed right away. This feels like one of those."

Bert reassured her softly. "We'll be cautious and check our six-o-clock frequently, Sweetheart, so don't worry. Take care of your Mom and do what you need to do there. She needs you with her to guide her to the next dimension. Be with her now. Later, I'll give you the complete rundown on what I'm doing here."

"Thanks for understanding, Bert, another reason why I love you. We'll get back in touch again soon, tomorrow evening hopefully." She began to cry. "Right now, my Mom needs me, Honey. She needs me, like I need you. I love her as I love you. How I miss your touch, Bert. Be careful."

She was gone. Bert sat upright, rubbed his forehead, and then hugged Missy, who had come to his chair. He knew she had sensed his conflicted and longing heart. He pressed his hands into her soft reddish-grey coat and felt her warmth. It helped calm his mind. After several minutes with his face and hands pressed against her thickening winter coat, he released her and stood up, looking out the window. This could be a lonely occupation sometimes, especially without Norah by his side. Then he looked at Missy, sitting on her haunches, looking directly at him, her sharp ears erect. For just a second, he was reminded of the way the Husky looked at him along the Yellowstone Highway. She yapped one time. It was an audible acknowledgment of his treasured existence by another living, breathing, creature. He wasn't alone. The loneliness began to subside and his logical mind began to come alive.

He took stock of the situation as it seemed to be unfolding. He was increasingly convinced that the young guard, Jeremy, wasn't the culprit. Right now, he considered the most likely rats to be the Police Chief and the older security guard, Kevin. One seemed driven by thirst for political power, the other by financial need. Could there be others, though? Was it remotely possible for Jim Atkins to betray his friend? Would a power-hungry Police Chief risk prison time for kidnapping, or worse, just to shave four years off his political ambitions? Would a guard risk it for a condition which could be handled by bankruptcy?

Then there's Norah's warning. Does that have anything to do with the guy and his dog that seem to be watching him? "Whoever that guy is, he's damn good!" thought Bert. "I've only seen him a couple times. If he's watching me full time, then he knows his craft. Pretty brazen, too, because he doesn't seem to care when I do see him. Just stands and looks at me, almost like he's taunting me."

Questions! Not any answers. Not yet, anyway. Tomorrow will be a new day. Missy had already taken her spot under the window, back in charge of security. Bert felt a calming sense of reassurance as he watched her chest softly heaving. "Good night, my little buddy," he whispered. Then he headed for the bed.

CHAPTER SIX: NARROWING THE FIELD

The rising sun was still a red glow in the eastern sky, brilliant in the 25-degree cold air on this Friday morning, October 6th, 2017. Bert and Missy arrived at the dirt road, which was only a five-minute drive from their motel. He opened the lift gate of the doghouse and summoned Missy to hop out. She did so with gusto and excitedly jumped and rubbed against his legs, then spinning in a couple of circles, and crouching as if to entice him to chase her. He closed the door and feigned a charge. She raced off, dirt flying as she tore a hundred yards up the road and then came tearing back. She was ready for this walk.

Bert strolled briskly along the dirt road, headed east toward the horizon of the coming sunrise. In the faint early morning light, he could see a few cows grazing in the adjacent pasture, against the backdrop of low grass covered hills. This eastern part of Wyoming was a part of the Great Plains, a portion of what the earliest discoverers called The Great American Desert. Little did they know that it would become one of the most productive cattle producing regions on the globe.

The green grasses of summer had given way to the dry brown grasses of the approaching winter. He inhaled deeply, taking in the life-giving cold air, and hiked his collar up a bit more against his neck. Early mornings were when he felt most alive. He chuckled as Missy sought to elicit a response from one of the nearby range cows. She always seemed to get a kick out of bothering a cow. He watched the large animal charge her a few times and marveled at the ease with which she stayed out of reach. He whistled for her to resume the walk, and she came running; done with that distraction, and ready for a new adventure.

Twenty minutes later, with the sun on their backs, Bert and

Missy arrived back at the car. Time to get the day started. He dialed Governor Patterson's number.

"Hello Governor, this is Cody. Calling to check in and see if you'd care to meet for a coffee after bit?"

Governor Patterson was anxious to meet, also. "You bet, Cody, how about we meet at the intersection prior to the west place; by the gas station. I know another little spot with good coffee and great pie. We can get it to go and sit in my car to talk. How does 8:30 work for you?"

Bert looked at his phone. It was 7:15. He would need to get moving if he was going to get across town in fifteen minutes to the intersection of the two interstate highways. "I'll be there, boss. See you outside the station."

Twenty-five minutes later, they walked out of Shari's Restaurant, a piece of pie and a coffee in hand. Bert entered the passenger side of the Governor's personal pickup as Sam got behind the wheel. They both took a long sip of coffee and had a first bite of their pie, before saying a word. Sam leaned back and gave a sigh. "Oh my God, thank God for coffee, and good pie! Haven't been sleeping worth a damn, Bert. I hope we can get Sammie home soon. Not sure how much more stress and worry I can take."

"Any word yet from the kidnappers?" Bert asked.

"No, nothing; not a word. That concerns me a lot, because we can only guess at their motive. I think I must give a press briefing today on her disappearance and ask for public help. Can't keep this quiet any longer. I'm thinking about 1:00 this afternoon."

Bert understood the growing fear building in this man, this father. "Yes Sir, I think it's time to do that, Governor. Maybe someone out there knows something. Even if not, the public can add their eyes and ears to the hunt for Sammie. Sam, I don't think that young guard, Jeremy, had anything to do with this."

The Governor looked Bert in the eyes. "Why do you think that, Bert, when all the evidence and opinions point to him?"

"He's the perfect fall guy for this, Sam. He was at your house, alone there much of the time with your daughter, responsible for security. Do you know if there's a TV in the foyer or near the entrance to your house?"

The Governor decided to entertain the idea. "Okay, let's talk about it. Yes, there's a television, a small flat screen, about 24 inches, I suppose, in the entry foyer. It was put there for guests who might have to wait to either enter or leave the property. Why?"

"Do you know who the UW Cowboys were playing last Saturday night, Governor?"

He thought about that for a few seconds. "Yes, I do. It was a big game for us. We were playing the Air Force Academy Falcons. We're one and two in the conference; at least we were before that game."

"Remember when that game started? Kickoff time?"

Sam thought a couple seconds. "Yeah, sure do. We were all recording it and hated to go to the Old Mansion event. It kicked off literally as we were walking out the door."

Bert continued his logic. "Do you know that one of your most staunch Cowboy fans, died-in-the-wool, is on your security staff? A guy who would rather miss dinner than a game."

"Let me guess. Jeremy Holland?" Governor Patterson could see where this was going.

"That's right, Governor," Bert went on, "The perfect fall guy was a known football fan, and a big game of the week was playing with his team. He's human and he's a young guy. Dedicated to his job and to you, but on that one night he kept sneaking peeks on the game. You know how that goes. Your minute turns into ten, and so on. Everything seemed quiet, so he spent more time than he should have checking on the game. He was derelict in his duty, Sam, and maybe he should be reassigned or fired; but I don't see him as a party to the kidnapping of your daughter. From what I've been learning, he probably even had a crush on her. He'd be the last one to hurt her, I think. Our mole is still out there."

Governor Patterson sat quietly, contemplating what Bert had said. Then he turned toward Bert. "Well, Bert, you might be right. I hated to think that Holland was the Judas, as I liked him. He seemed like a nice young guy; Sammie liked him too. So, what next?"

Bert knew this question was coming. "I think we just keep an eye on Jeremy but let him keep working there. Better to have him close than out of sight, if we're wrong about him. In the meantime, unless something else develops, there are others better to focus on. One is your Chief of Police. How badly do you think he wants your job?"

Governor Patterson wasn't surprised by that question. "The Chief is known to be an egotistical ass sometimes, and power hungry. I know he has higher aspirations, which at least include Governor of the State of Wyoming. So, the question is would he risk everything to kidnap my daughter to get me to quit and not run for re-election? What would be his exit strategy?"

Bert thought for a minute. "Sam, part of the answer to this line of thought is whether this kidnapping might make you either resign early or choose to not run for a second term? If Sammie isn't found soon, or God forbid at all, would you continue as Governor, or go on to a second term? From all accounts, you're a shoo-in for re-election. Could you be essentially forced out of the Statehouse by this awful event?"

Governor Samuel Patterson leaned back in the driver's seat, and dropped his head against the head rest, his eyes open but unseeing. He inhaled deeply and let it out slowly. "Bert, I've been thinking about this for the past couple of days. This is hitting me, and Betsy, so hard that we're both struggling just to get through the day. The nights are unbearable. As soon as I announce Sammie's disappearance today, I will at least be able to legitimately take some time off and people will understand. So far, I've had to create the façade of business as usual. To answer your question honestly, Bert, I don't see how I could continue as Governor if we don't get our daughter back. I'm not sure I could finish this term, much less run for another next year. I think I would have to turn it over to the Lieutenant Governor."

Bert was leaning back in the passenger seat, as well, listening intently. He was not surprised by what this man and father was saying. "Sam, I understand what you're saying. Most fathers would say the same thing, I believe. From the standpoint of my investigation, I can assume that political motivation is a possible motive. The goal of this kidnapping may not be money, at all; it could be to force you out of office. That might explain the lack of any demands."

Bert brought up the other key suspect, Kevin, the other security guard. "For Kevin Murphy, the motive could be money. He's on the verge of going under, financially, from all reports. He would need help, though, and those people might be driven by politics. Given the high risk of going to prison, why wouldn't he just bite the bullet and go bankrupt? That's not the end of the world."

He continued. "Sam, how are you, financially? Are you well enough off that your money could be the goal for kidnapping?

Sam was fast to answer. "I'm doing okay, Bert. My business has been successful. I'm not made of money, though. I'd be hard pressed to come up with two million bucks, and that would mean selling off a bunch of assets. Two million is chump change to most kidnappers. I'd have to rely upon the good will and help from a lot of other folks to get much more than that. My finances are pretty much a matter of public record, so any informed criminal could be aware of that."

"One other thing," Bert asked. "Did you notice anyone parked on the street at the end of your driveway as you left your house last Saturday?"

The Governor leaned forward against the steering wheel, resting his forehead on it. After about fifteen seconds, he leaned back and turned toward Bert. "You know, we were in a hurry after Sammie's injury, so I didn't pay much attention to the route. I'm not sure, but there may have been a car parked there. I can't say for sure. It isn't all that unusual to see cars parked along that street, though not all the time. Maybe Betsy remembers?"

"If you don't mind, would you ask her about that when you think it's appropriate? It might be helpful if we know that detail."

Bert felt this was a good place to wrap it up for now. He didn't want to add more to this man's stress than was already there. "Sam, unless you have more you want to discuss, how about we go from here? I'll continue to look into the two men we've discussed, keep an eye on Jeremy, and see what other political things might surface. I hope the press conference goes well. Would it be okay if

I attend, in the background of course?"

Sam was obviously struggling with all this. "Yes, it's okay for you to attend the press conference, covertly. It'll be on the steps of the Capitol."

"I like this place, and that pie is to die for," Bert exclaimed. "How about Shari's Restaurant becomes our 'Dessert Central' from now on? And, yes, I will be at the Capitol conference."

Governor Patterson agreed as he drove Bert back to where they left his vehicle. They said a quick good-bye and Bert returned to Missy, while Sam drove off to a Capitol position that no longer seemed very important.

Missy was whining and moving about in the car, sure signs that she needed a relief break. So, Bert drove a short way out of Cheyenne to a rural road, where he and Missy could take a fifteen-minute stroll and he could collect his thoughts.

As they walked along the dusty dirt road, Bert kept Missy close by to prevent anyone from mistaking her for one of her wild cousins. He didn't want her to get shot as she meandered along the fence line, checking out the bunch grass and gopher mounds, seeing if a snack might be lurking. He never tired of watching her doing her coyote thing, and marveling at her increasingly luxurious winter coat.

Bert knew he needed to be incognito at the press conference, and decided on a sports coat, blue jeans, hiking boots, and a felt winter cap with sunglasses. He'd try to get close to the Police Chief and hear whatever he could. Likewise, if possible, anything he could learn about Jim Atkins would be a good thing. Between now and the press conference, he'd go back to the motel and get online. It's time to follow up on his skill in becoming a friend to several

Facebook and Twitter accounts and see what conversations are taking place.

* * *

Under a clear blue sky, with no wind and a 38-degree temperature, great for Wyoming in October, Governor Samuel Patterson walked down the steps of the State Capitol to face the small throng of reporters and spectators. This would be the shortest press briefing of his tenure in office.

He cleared his throat and began. "Thank you all for coming on such short notice. This will be very brief, and I will not be taking questions. You'll understand why, I think. My Lieutenant Governor, Bill Vandersloff, will remain to answer some of your questions. Also, Police Chief, Brian Holcomb, can update you on his involvement to date. Last Saturday night, September 30th, my sixteen-year-old daughter, Samantha, known as Sammie, was abducted from our Governor's Residence around seven that evening while my wife, Betsy, and I were at an event at the Old Governor's Mansion. We kept this matter private until now in the hopes that developments might more readily lead to her return. To date, we've had no communications with the abductors, and the motive is not known. We'll appreciate any information the public may already have, may suspect, or might learn, if it helps us get Sammie back home. Betsy and I ask that you respect our privacy and work with our designated officials for further information. Thank you all for coming." With that, Governor Patterson walked down the steps to a waiting staff car, which would take him home to be with his wife and other visiting family.

Bert had positioned himself near the front side of the group of reporters, with a clear view of the next speaker, Police Chief Holcomb, whom the Lieutenant Governor had deferred to. He listened intently to the Chief's replies to the many questions. Several caught his keen interest.

"Chief Holcomb," asked a reporter from the Star-Tribune, "Do you have any good leads or suspects at this time?"

"Absolutely," replied Holcomb with an air of authority, "We have a couple of solid suspects and we are actively investigating both."

The girl from the Laramie Boomerang wanted to know if the Governor would continue in office if Sammie wasn't found soon.

Holcomb was quick to answer. "We aren't thinking about that. We're focused on getting his daughter back, as soon as possible and alive. Nothing else matters right now."

The Wyoming Tribune Eagle reporter asked, "There are rumors that you might run for Governor if Governor Patterson decides not to stay in office or run for a second term. Are you considering that, Chief?"

"Down the road, when Governor Patterson is no longer planning to serve, I have been asked to consider running for Governor. However, that's not the current concern. Right now, I'm a faithful servant of our Governor."

"Well, he does have all the right answers," thought Bert.

The Tribune Eagle reporter asked again, "Chief, if the Governor decides to resign from his office as a result of his daughter's kidnapping, do you intend to begin campaigning for his job at next year's election?"

"First things first, folks," replied Chief Holcomb sternly. "The most important thing right now is to do everything possible to bring the Governor's daughter back home safely. After that, we'll consider all options based upon the situation."

"So, he is thinking about running for Governor, even now as the search for Sammie continues," Bert surmised. He noticed another few reporters gathering around Jim Atkins, who was off to the far side of the crowd, listening to the speakers. Bert quietly moved through the crowd until he could hear the discussions with Jim. He knew Jim was not likely to recognize him in his disguise of colored glasses, thick mustache, winter sports coat, and winter cap. The clipboard and recorder in his hands made him look like any other media reporter.

"No, I appreciate your question, but the Governor's my friend and my complete focus is on helping him and his wife get through this trying time." Jim Atkins seemed a little perplexed by the question. "I have said to the Governor before that when his second and final term of office is over, then I would consider following in his footsteps and helping continue his legacy of service to Wyoming."

Another small-town newsman asked, "You're a close friend and confidant, Mr. Atkins. Do you think Governor Patterson will resign if his daughter isn't found soon?"

Bert could tell that Jim was trying to control his anger. "Listen, folks, I know you guys love to speculate on these things, but this is not helpful to anyone. I think all of us should be focusing entirely upon helping get this family's child back. Political decisions will take care of themselves at the appropriate times. These are our friends, and when they suffer, we suffer. Thanks for your questions. I'm not taking any more at this time."

Bert worked his way around the crowd and toward the administrative building a block away. He was less concerned about Jim Atkins as a possible suspect, not totally off the hook, but not so skewered by it as before. This being a Friday, he needed to investigate some official documents before the weekend made it no longer possible.

Inside the Records Division, Bert had to show his identity in order to get the documents he wanted to review. He had to wait a few minutes in line and ahead of several others, apparently there to beat the Friday rush, also.

"There you go, Mr. Lynnes, these are the upcoming issues and bills before the House and Senate over the foreseeable year." The clerk was surprisingly cheery for having to spend nearly fifteen minutes fulfilling his request. "You can use the small room over near that corner to review them. Just return them here when you're finished to get your ID back."

Bert thanked her and maneuvered his way around the three other people, two men dressed in business suits, and a woman dressed professionally in a green pants suit. He apologized as he moved between two of them and into the small waiting room. Once inside, he began the tedious task of trying to list the upcoming legislation which would likely end up before the Governor during the next twelve months. After twenty minutes, he knew he had only enough time to list those which seemed particularly significant.

With five minutes to go before the office closed, Bert returned the documents to the clerk, picked up his ID, thanked her, and nodded to the one man still frantically racing the clock to complete his research. At the stroke of 5:00 PM, he exited the building, followed closely by the remaining businessman and the clerk. He walked back to his car and Missy. She would be more than ready to get out. He drove back out of town, past his motel, to the road they had walked at sunrise. It was time to reward Missy's patience in the car with a good walk. After that, it's time to talk with Norah.

* * *

"Bert, you won't believe what just happened a few hours ago," Norah exclaimed excitedly. "Mom's awake! The doctors said there was no hope, but she just woke up."

Bert was shocked. "Oh my God, are you serious, darling? She's out of the coma? How'd that happen, babe, do they know? I mean, that's great news, Sweetheart. I'm so surprised, but I'm happy for all of you."

"I know," she replied excitedly, "It's a miracle, Bert. The medical community had given up on her and basically said she was dying and nothing more could be done. She's not out of the woods, though, as she will still need recovery care. However, it looks now like she might be going home in a few days. My sister is going to stay with her for that period. So, I'll be able to come back with you very soon. I can't wait to be there and get into your case with you."

"I'm anxious to have you back here, too. However, take your time and stay near Mom for as long as you think you need to. Just continue to give me a reading now and then if you're picking up any vibes from here. That can be very helpful to me." Bert knew she'd take a minute and give him a quick reading.

Norah was quiet for a couple minutes. Finally, she offered Bert the things that were coming to her. "Honey, as I said before, be very careful! Something has changed, maybe just today. The vision of the fox, rabbit, and wolf, which I told you about yesterday is different. In my vision just now, the fox is stalking the rabbit, but now the wolf is already stalking the fox. The wolf has become aware of you, darling. You are now the prey. I sense that you are in grave danger. Are you sure you want to continue with this case?"

Bert sat in stunned and reflective silence for over two minutes, digesting her words and reliving his activities of the day. Where was the wolf and how did it discover him? Did that man and his dog figure out what I'm here to do? Have they just been watching me so far to see if I'm getting on the trail? "I'll be extremely careful, Sweetheart. I'm trying to figure out what happened today which may have disclosed my reason for being in Cheyenne. Anything else, Sweetheart?"

She didn't answer right away, again. "Well, I'm still seeing that 104 number, and still have no idea what it means. It must be significant, though. The most unsettling thing to me is that I'm catching glimpses of you, through a scope. We've hunted together before, so I know what a target looks like through a gun scope. I see you in a circle, with cross hairs on you, Bert. This is chilling, because it feels like someone is going to shoot at you, Honey. I'm very scared for you!"

He leaned back in his chair, eyes closed, and mind racing. "Thanks, Honey, I'm going to think back on my tracks today and try to figure out where I may have crossed paths with the wrong person. I promise you that I'll be as careful as possible, so please don't worry. Knowledge is power, Sweetheart, and your insight gives me the edge. I'm very happy about the good turn for your Mom. Have a good evening, Norah. Good night."

With good-byes said, Bert leaned forward, motioned for Missy, and wrapped his arms around her chest. He laid his face against the thickening hair on her neck, closed his eyes, and just enjoyed the sense of peace emanating from her warm, living body. How he missed putting his arms around his wife and getting that feeling from her warmth. His tears sifted down through Missy's soft reddish-grey coat, as pent up emotions released. Missy stood quietly while Bert's sense of loneliness and inner grief connected with her soul. She seemed to understand that her alpha male needed her right now.

CHAPTER SEVEN: NOTHING MUCH OBVIOUS

Saturday, October 7th, dawned to another clear and chilly day, as Bert and Missy walked along the outlying dirt road a few miles from their motel. The red glow in the eastern sky foretold the coming of the sun. The frost on the grasses and barbed wire provided a visual reminder of the thirty degrees temperature. With absolutely no wind, it looked like this would be a great fall day. A great day for college football!

Missy trotted down the road a hundred yards in front of him, barely visible in the still dim light of approaching sunrise. She was ever attentive to her surroundings, stopping frequently to cock her head and listen to sounds of gathering morning. In the distance, one of her wild cousins was initiating what would become a yapping chorus for twenty or thirty seconds. Missy raised her muzzle to the dark sky and returned their greeting. In the darkness, her first two yaps evolved into a long soul filling and melancholy howl. Then another and another. The cacophony would end just as abruptly as it began, as if on an instinctive cue. After that, silence.

A sadness came over Bert, as he couldn't help but wonder if she missed her kind. Was her vocalization a token of a primitive longing for canine companionship? If so, he understood, because he too, sometimes felt the urge to cry to the darkness for those things lost and so unattainable. Just as Missy missed the companionship of her wild cousins, so he missed the warm and tender touch of his wife. How he longed to just hold her in his arms and feel her heart beat. He wiped tears from his cheeks before they froze.

They resumed walking. There was just the sound of their feet shuffling down the sandy road. A mile later, Bert turned them around and back toward the vehicle as the rising sunlight gave welcome warmth on their backs. It was time to get to work on the plan he had arrived at last night.

After his talk with Norah, Bert had stayed up several more hours, resuming his survey of the internet media, connected to several of the players, in this hunt for clues. One of his discoveries was that Jim Atkins' wife, Andrea, was an avid reader, loved books, and loved attending a Saturday morning book club meeting in the back room of a Laramie coffee shop. This morning they were going to review and discuss a documentary, which Bert knew he would find interesting. It would also be an opportunity to maybe gain some insight into the Atkins, especially Andrea. Some things were nagging at him about her, and he felt the need to learn more about her. He and Missy hustled back to the motel, had breakfast, and prepared to head west on Interstate 80 toward Laramie. Missy took her usual place in the cargo area, ready for a snooze.

Disguised with a thick salt-and-pepper mustache, extended sideburns, leather jacket, moderate rimmed glasses, and a winter ball cap, Bert walked into the meeting of the Laramie Readers Club just a minute or two after it started. As it turned out, Andrea was doing the initial review of their chosen book and she was at the podium. It was a documentary by an investigative reporter out of Denver into a serial murder case which recently concluded. Bert knew he would find it interesting; the title was "The Nickel Dime Murders of Big Sky Country."

Following Andrea's review, numerous questions and inputs ensued from the fifty or so in attendance. Most were women, but there were roughly a dozen men there also, including Bert. After a few minutes, one of the ladies turned to Bert, in his position at the back of the room. "I believe we have a guest today," she said, "Sir, can you stand and tell us what brings you to our club this morning?"

Bert stood up, nodded to the group, and quickly gathered his thoughts. "Good morning and thanks for allowing me to attend your meeting. I'm Cody Winslow. This has been interesting, just as I thought it would be when I stumbled upon your website last night. I'm passing through the area, staying over the weekend, and love reading and learning. So here I am. I'm interested in the politics of Wyoming, especially the upcoming race for Governor. I hoped I might learn some about that, too, from you folks. I'm thinking of doing a freelance article about this election next year."

"Well you came to the right place for that, Cody," the lady continued. "We have a future First Lady of Wyoming in our midst, and she's still at the podium. Meet Andrea Atkins, one day to be the wife of our Governor." A murmur of chuckles and laughs rippled across the room.

Andrea was quick to come back to her fellow readers. "Mr. Winslow, Cody if I may, these people are just jealous because they aren't married to someone with the talent, skills, and connections to become Governor. However, sir, I am married to such a man and I know he will follow in the footsteps of his friend, Samuel Patterson. Obviously, this will be after Governor Patterson's term of office has ended."

Another lady put in her two cents worth. "Don't let her fool you, Cody, if she could will her husband into the Governor's chair tomorrow, she'd do it. She's destined to live in the Governors' Residence." Again, laughter emanated around the room. It seemed to be good natured and friendly, though, Bert thought.

"Now you all know that we're friends with the Patterson family. And, this is a very serious and trying time for them, with the disappearance of their daughter." Andrea was no longer glib but seemed genuinely serious. "I would not trade ten terms as a Governor's wife for Sammie's safe return." There were no snickers now, but just nods of agreement from the group. Levity was replaced with a sense of genuine concern.

Bert sat down and listened to a few more minutes of this solemn discussion about what might have happened to Sammie Patterson. Just as Andrea was about to leave the podium, a woman entered from outside the room, went to her hurriedly, and whispered something into her ear. It was apparently unsettling, because the look on Andrea's face changed to a greater expression of concern. She returned to her chair near the front of the group.

After the meeting, Bert wanted to get closer to Mrs. Atkins, but she left the meeting with only a few salutations to those closest to her. Bert had to settle for a chat with one of the other ladies, obviously one of the leaders. "I enjoyed Mrs. Atkins' review. She evidently really believes her husband is destined to become Governor. I couldn't help but notice that she seemed concerned about something as she left so quickly. Is everything okay with her and her family?"

This woman was eager to talk with him. "Oh, she is very serious about her husband and his aspirations; her aspirations, too. She's a political animal, loves it, and there's no doubt that she'd love to be a First Lady. Maybe of more than just Wyoming." She laughed at that. "She always meets up with her son, who is a student at UW, on Saturday mornings for breakfast at the Sweet Melissa. It's one of Laramie's, and Wyoming's, best restaurants. Apparently, they haven't heard from their son for a while. She just has a mother's worry; he's probably just recovering from a big date and hasn't gotten up yet."

"I know how it is to worry about someone," Bert sympathized,

"I hope everything is alright." With that he said his thanks and good-byes to the key players in the room and departed. Maybe it'd be a good idea to get some breakfast, he thought.

Bert changed into a different jacket and a felt western hat, during an en route stop on the way to the Sweet Melissa restaurant. The subtle change should be enough to keep Andrea from noticing him. He enjoyed the crisp, clear beauty of this perfect fall day. Bert really loved this quaint little cow and college town, nestled in a mountain pass and valley. It was home to so many neat businesses as well as the University of Wyoming. There was always the feel of an old west town, but with the hustle and undercurrent of excitement that comes with college students.

Once inside the Sweet Melissa, he chose a table across the room from where Mrs. Atkins was sitting, alone. He ordered his breakfast and continued to glance at Andrea as she drank her coffee and eventually began to eat alone. There was a worried look on her face. She finished her meal about the time that Bert was finishing a third cup of coffee, and reluctantly departed the restaurant. "I wonder what's going on with her family." He thought to himself.

As he drove thoughtfully toward Cheyenne on Interstate 80, Bert decided to give Missy another outing, as well as be unpredictable to anyone keeping tabs on them. At Buford, he took the exit for Curt Gowdy State Park. This park would likely be almost vacant, just as was the Vedauwoo Park. Besides some serenity, pretty scenery, and some good walking trails, it would be a good place to do some thinking. Named for the legendary Wyoming sports radio broadcaster and personality, this park represented the best of Wyoming's natural beauty and fishing.

* * *

Once inside the Gowdy State Park, Bert turned into a parking area near the North Crow Reservoir. He noted there were no other visitors on this chilly October day, and let Missy out. She danced around his legs excitedly, turning in circles, and whining; ready to get on a trail. Before they started walking, though, Bert did a careful and thorough survey of his surroundings, looking for any signs of Norah's wolf. He did not doubt that it was out there, somewhere. Seeing nothing of concern, he and Missy started down the trail.

This would be a time when his attention was not on the scenery. His mind was methodically going down the issues and questions. The first major question was what happened yesterday to sic the wolf on him? Did someone at the Governor's press conference notice and recognize him? He tried to stroll through that event in his mind, and nothing stood out as unusual. Another possibility was at "Dessert Central," Shari's Restaurant, yesterday morning with Sam. Could he or they have been followed there? Were they being watched as they sat in Sam's truck? He simply didn't know. He didn't notice anyone, but that wouldn't be unusual if a professional investigator was involved. What else?

Then it struck him. There were three business looking people at the records office in the afternoon. He had to use his real name and ID in order to get the records he needed. Those in line or even in the office could have heard his name. If they were familiar with his background, it would not be too difficult to put two and two together. If that's where he was compromised, then his intuition in being there might be on point. Something in those records could point to the wolf, the real reason for Sammie's abduction.

Then there's the question about the motivation of the Governor's friends, the Atkins. After listening to Jim after the press conference, his gut instinct told him that Jim was not likely to betray his friend, Sam Patterson. However, another possibility was gelling

73

in his mind after the morning book club meeting. Was it possible that Jim's wife, Andrea, could be the force tying the kidnapping together? She seems to be politically motivated, even more so than her husband. She was among the first at the old Historic Mansion last Saturday night to know about Sammie's injury and staying home. She's known to have made at least two phone calls back to her home, the first upon learning of Sammie's change in plans. Supposedly she left a message on their home phone when she didn't reach her son. Was someone else there waiting for a message? Where was their son, Andrew? Clearly, Andrea could be the judas. The question though, was she?

Before he moved on to the next issue, Bert couldn't help but wonder what was going on after the meeting this morning. Obviously, there was concern about the Atkins' son, Andrew. Andrea was identifiably upset at the planned breakfast meeting when he didn't show. "I need to find out about this," Bert said aloud.

He jolted back to reality. Where's Missy? He'd lost sight of her in this rural, unimproved reservoir fishing setting. After a couple of increasingly anxious minutes, he spotted her near the edge of the reservoir, bounding in the tall water grasses. She was onto something out there, probably something that might be good to eat. She reluctantly sidled toward him in typical coyote gait, looking back to the water even as she returned to her master. She was not ready to give up on an afternoon snack.

With Missy safely near him again and back on the trail, Bert turned his thoughts back to his media investigations. Police Chief Holcomb had an active involvement on Facebook and a law enforcement blog. One of his "friends" was a man referred to as "Jess." When Bert found Jess' accounts, they were nearly devoid of personal information, work history, and so forth. Jess' last name was listed as "Palm." During some of their conversations, though, the initials "FP" came up a few times, and seemed to be related to a business that Jess related to. Weeks back, there was a brief exchange about Jess' time working for a large medical supplier. The bulk of their chat was so nondescript that it could almost be taken as code, thought Bert. Other than that, there was very little to be suspicious about.

Jeremy Holland was understandably wise and saying very little on his media accounts. He sounded like a man who knows his every move is being observed.

Kevin Murphy, the security guard with money problems, wasn't as good at zipping his lip. He was doing plenty of complaining about being nearly wiped out financially over all kinds of things. He exuded the despair that seemed to accompany financial ruin. No hint of anything sinister, though.

"Time to head back to Cheyenne," Bert thought to himself. He whistled for Missy and they turned back toward the doghouse. On the brisk return walk, Bert relaxed his mind from the mysteries of the case and let himself enjoy the scenery and the fresh air. He needed the break now, because there would be plenty of concerns back in Cheyenne.

As he drove east on the Happy Jack road toward Cheyenne, in keeping with throwing off any surveillance, he contemplated his next move. "I need to call the Governor, I think. It's been over a day since he announced the disappearance of his daughter. Maybe there's been some development." He looked back to see if Missy was listening and approved. She raised her head from where she lay and looked at him, yawned, stretched, and proceeded to go back to sleep. "Well, I think it's a good idea, anyway," he scolded her. She still didn't seem to care.

As he drove along Happy Jack, he called Governor Patterson. He identified himself as Cody and asked if he had time to meet at the west place in two hours. The Governor agreed. He'd be there in an hour.

* * *

Governor Patterson arrived at the west place bar and restaurant about ten minutes ahead of Bert. The unimproved road took a little longer than Bert expected. It was almost five on a Saturday afternoon, and the UW game with Colorado State was about to kickoff. The place was very crowded. "Maybe that wasn't a bad thing," Sam thought.

It took Bert a couple of minutes to find Sam in the back corner of the crowded room and bar. He had his previous western look, so wasn't easy to spot in the throng of Wyoming cowboys. "Howdy, Sam," he said, "looks like we'll be hiding in plain sight and lost in the crowd in here.

Sam nodded in agreement. "What's new? Have you discovered anything more for us to go on?"

"Sam, I can't say yet if I'm onto anything or not. I have discovered some interesting things regarding some of the suspects, but it doesn't confirm anyone. I wanted to ask you one thing, Sir. Do you know if there is anything going on with the Atkins' son?"

Sam seemed a little surprised by the question. "Well, there is a new development, Bert. If you remember, their son Andrew lives off campus. He shares an apartment with another guy, who works locally, not a student. Jim and Andrea haven't seen their son now in nearly a week, and they just recently became alarmed that they can't seem to get in touch with him."

"Really! Does the roommate have any ideas about Andrew's whereabouts? Didn't they suspect something sooner than now?" Bert was a bit confused.

"Jim told me today that Andrew was upset about Sammie's disappearance last Saturday, and on Sunday when Andrea last saw him. Andrew sometimes just goes into the mountains and camps for a few days when he gets upset. So, his parents didn't think too much about it until the past two days. They knew he was close to Sammie and very upset by her abduction. The roommate doesn't know where he might be. He said that Andrew just left last Sunday, and he hadn't seen him since. Jim and Andrea thought their son was either attending classes or out in the mountains; and they were being very supportive of Betsy and me. They just didn't worry about him for several days."

Bert thought about all that for a few seconds as he sipped a beer with Sam. "What you're telling me, Sam, is that we may have two abductions going on. Your daughter and Atkins' son. What would be the common thread, though? Jim is no threat politically, at least not yet. Is he?"

Sam was also quietly pondering the questions. "Damned if I can see any link with those two kids. Sammie yes, but not Andrew. It makes no sense."

"Could Andrew's disappearance just be a weird coincidence; suspicious timing but otherwise not related to Sammie?" Bert was openly perplexed by this development. "Are the cops onto this case, yet, Sam; if so, have they interviewed the roommate?"

"Jim and Andrea just filed a missing person report late yesterday with the Laramie police. They did send someone to interview the roommate, his name is Larue something. Boynton, I think. He's a traveling salesman for one of the big pharmaceutical companies.

He claims to know nothing."

Bert was curious. "If Larue isn't a student, how did he and Andrew hook up to rent an apartment together. I thought Jim said that Andrew lived on campus when we first talked?"

"Yeah, the boy was on campus until just a few weeks ago. Jim said that his son met Larue at one of the local college hangouts, and they hit if off to the point that Larue asked if Andrew would like to share an apartment with him. It was about half the cost of the dorm, and Larue was gone a lot. A pretty good deal for Andrew, who likes his privacy, and is frugal with his money. Andrew is working and paying part of his way through college. Jim and Andrea insisted on that." Sam had obviously discussed a lot of this with his friend, Jim.

"Sam, let's continue to talk about these developments at least once a day," Bert stated matter-of-factly. "My gut tells me there's a connection, though I can't see what the hell it could be, right now. I need to tell you something else, too."

"What's that?" Sam wanted to know.

Bert leaned closer to his client and friend. "Sam, my psychic believes that I've somehow been compromised. We can only guess about how that may have happened. She thinks I'm in danger. I'm telling you this in case something happens, but I'm being very cautious."

"If that's so, Bert, then it tells me that something you've done, are doing, or are likely to do, has raised suspicions. You're a threat to those who did this. You need to be careful, Bert. Maybe we should bring you out of the dark and into the light, let my staff know you're working for me?" Sam was concerned about Bert's safety.

Bert didn't want to do that just yet and asked Sam to hold off on that decision for now. He felt he could still be more valuable working undercover. "There is one thing you can do for me, though." Bert asked. "Would you have someone on your staff go by the records office and get a list of everyone, which will include me, who conducted any business there Friday afternoon. I'm not sure what I'm looking for just yet, but that might help me narrow it down. Include sign in and out times."

The Governor didn't think twice. "You bet, Bert, I'll have one of my staffers get on it first thing Monday. Should have it for you no later than noon. You suspect that you were somehow compromised there, I gather?"

"Yup, I think that's a distinct possibility, Sam. I had to use my real name and identification in order to get the documents I wanted to review. There were a couple of people in the line, as well as the clerk. It's a long shot, but one of them might work with the wolf."

"The wolf?" asked Sam.

Bert chuckled. "Sorry, yeah, my psychic refers to the bad guy as the wolf. She believes the wolf is aware of me after yesterday. Something I did or said tipped someone off, if she's right. Unfortunately, Sam, she's usually right."

The Governor laughed nervously. "Okay, I can relate to that analogy. Let's hope she's wrong. I don't feel good about you being in danger. So be careful and tell me if you want to come out or get protection."

"I'll let you know, Sam. For now, I think we'll be most effective if I stay off the grid as long as I can. There may be some benefit from the element of surprise. Letting the wolf think he hasn't been seen might be a benefit."

Sam leaned back and watched the next play in the game. It turned out to be a 24-yard pass completion by Wyoming to the Ram's 12-yard line. "Damn, Bert, if we score here, we'll be tied with 10 minutes until half. I haven't watched football in too long. How about we watch this game until half, and then I'm going back home. I could use a short break from the rest of life. And yes, I agree with you."

Bert gladly turned his full attention to the game. A football fan in general, Bert was also a fan of the Cowboys. "You got it, boss. I could use a diversion myself. It's hard trying to live inside your own head this much. I need some external stimulation. Some Wyoming football can fill the bill."

Both men let out a yell along with the rest of the crowd. Wyoming scored on a 12-yard misdirection run. Game tied!

* * *

"Hi Norah, how are you and how's Mom tonight?" Bert was animated because he was still watching the game in his motel room and it was tied entering the fourth quarter. He hit the pause button when Norah contacted him.

"Hi Bert, Honey, Mom is continuing to make a miraculous recovery. The family is elated. It looks like she may go home tomorrow. If that works out, Sweetheart, I'll be with you again on Monday. I'm very happy right now about all this! I can't wait to be back with you. I've so missed being with you, Bert."

Bert was overjoyed. "I am so thrilled about all that, my love. I've missed having you around. I'm glad your mother is doing so unbelievably well. That's just amazing! A real miracle."

"How is your case coming, darling?" Are you any closer to solving it? You've been on it about a week now, haven't you? I hope you're being very vigilant after what my vision told me."

"Yeah, I'm being cautious, Sweetheart. I take your visions seriously. Even discussed it with my, or rather our, client this afternoon. He wants me to be careful, also, but understands the continued need to stay low profile. Are you picking up any other inputs to share with me about this case? When you get here, I'll fill you in on as many of the details as you want."

She took her time replying, as was her usual method. "Bert, the only thing coming to me tonight, and I hope it makes sense to you, is like a message or a caution: 'Just because it's obvious, it doesn't make it right.'"

"Hmmm," he muttered. "That could apply to so many aspects of this case, Norah, the question becomes which aspect of it? That's all that's come to you tonight then?"

"Yes, I'm afraid so, Honey," she replied, "Maybe it's just because of all the new developments with Mom. Once I'm there with you, I should get more clarity and insight into what you're up against. For now, Bert, please just be careful. The wolf vision continues to be strong and clear. I better get back to Mom, Sweetheart. I love you and you have a good night. You're the captain of my ship."

"I love you, too, and I'm very glad your mother is doing this well, Norah. Good night, my first mate." With that, he turned back to the game. Wyoming was now up by 3 points with ten minutes left in the game. While he tried to stay entirely focused on the remaining game, his mind kept drifting to Norah's caution. "Just because it's obvious, it doesn't make it right." What does that pertain to?

CHAPTER EIGHT: RUNAWAYS

After their usual early morning jaunt, Bert and Missy returned to their motel. They had walked the entire way without taking the doghouse. He decided to add another precaution into his routine and another teaching moment for Missy. He called her close, got on his hands and knees at the side of the vehicle, and proceeded to get down and look underneath while smelling the vehicle up and down. He repeated over and over: "search, Missy; search, Missy."

She didn't get it at first and thought it a grand game. She crawled up to him on her belly, licked his face as he peered under the car, then rolled onto her back and kicked like a coyote on smack, whining and yapping. It took several attempts to get her to realize they were looking for something. A well-placed treat under the vehicle started to get her thinking right. By the time he got around to the back bumper of the car, repeating the command to search, she was crawling along with him, whimpering and whining with anticipation. Bert hoped nobody would see them in the parking lot, a man and a coyote crawling on their bellies around a vehicle. He'd either be arrested or taken away in a straight jacket.

Finally, she found the ball cap, which he had "borrowed" from the motel coat rack. Once she finished shaking the snot out of it, he managed to retrieve it, none the worse for coyote slobber. The rightful owner would never know his contribution to their safety. He laughed out loud as he rewarded her effort with a venison snack. She contained her desire for as long as she could, then with a yap she lunged and grabbed the treat from his outstretched hand.

Passing the coat rack, Bert glanced around to see if anyone was watching. He quickly wiped Missy's slobbers onto his pants leg and put the cap back on a peg. Crime over. Back inside their room, while Missy ate her breakfast and Bert mixed up his favorite smoothie, he resumed his online searching. He decided to try to find more about the Police Chief's friend, Jess Palm. Searching through Facebook and other blogs, he started to run across several Jess and Jessie Palmers. Was Jess Palm a code name for Jess or Jessie Palmer? One of those guys sometimes referred to where he worked: FP. "What the heck is FP," Bert thought.

He looked through the yellow pages online, for businesses starting with the letter F. While there were many, he couldn't find any in Cheyenne with a second name starting in P. "Damn," he said aloud, "I don't want to spend too much time on this in case it isn't significant, but how do I know if it is or isn't?" What next?

It was Sunday, October 8th, late mid-morning. Not much chance of doing anything official at the capitol. Also, he didn't want to disturb Governor Patterson and family on a Sunday morning, so he took out his notes from his visit to the records office on Friday. He had looked for upcoming legislation which would probably end up before the Governor within the next year. Maybe there was a clue there?

The first, House Bill 89, provided for greater regulation over feedlots across the state. This could be a bill of interest to many.

House Bill 101 would provide increased regulation over the way grazing permits were issued and managed on state-controlled lands. Certainly, this would be a hot button issue in an agricultural state. It would hit the Governor's desk probably early next year. Would Patterson sign it? Maybe?

The next, House Bill 102, was intended to provide greater definition as to what constituted a wetland in Wyoming, and how the resultant regulatory restrictions would apply to each category. Such restrictive regulations rarely set well with many farmers and ranchers.

House Bill 121 provided for the way bidding was to be accepted and processed for the selling of state assets, land, and other related state properties. Was that a significant thing to Wyoming? What kind of money was involved?

Then there was House Bill 112, which would provide greater restrictions upon the way abortions were performed and reported in Wyoming and provided for more state oversight. This is a state with the smallest population in the nation. Would such regulation really matter that much to those providers?

Finally, the last bill of significance that Bert could identify in the time he had Friday, was House Bill 104. This would also be a controversial issue, because it sought to provide greater regulatory oversight on the coal industry. Wyoming is one of the nation's top producers of coal, much of which fuels the power plants in the eastern US. It could be a big deal to those involved.

Bert fixed another coffee and propped his chair back against the desk, watching Missy, and thinking about these respective issues. They were all likely to hit Governor Patterson's desk within months, surely prior to the election next November. Would he support and sign them? "There's only one way to know," he said to Missy. "I have to ask him."

They needed another break from the motel, so Bert decided to take a drive down to the Terry Bison Ranch, about a half hour south of Cheyenne. On a Sunday it would be mostly closed but they could probably still walk around the old-time town and campgrounds. This was a very diverse operation, having a working buffalo ranch integrated with a tourism operation, and even a winery. It should be a good outing for both him and Missy.

The underbelly inspection of the vehicle went better, and Missy seemed to be catching on to a new responsibility. She alerted on the paper plate he had asked another motel patron to toss under the side and received another treat for her effort. Before entering the car, he slowly observed the entire 360 degrees around their parking, for anything suspicious. He didn't see anything of interest.

They entered Interstate highway 25, heading south toward Colorado. Within ten minutes, Cheyenne was disappearing in the rear-view mirror as they topped the first hill to the south. There were only a few other vehicles on the highway, a slow Sunday. Two of those vehicles were behind Bert, slowly overtaking him.

The first to pass him was a white sedan. It was going quite fast and quickly distanced itself toward the next low hill. The second was an older, dirty brown pickup, also overtaking him easily. It entered Bert's blind spot on the left side of the doghouse. Bert's eyes were on his rearview mirrors as was his habit whenever other vehicles were behind him.

"What the hell?" Bert let out a startled shout. The pickup had suddenly swerved toward Bert's left front wheel fender. Instinctively, Bert both slammed on his brake and took to the shoulder of the road. He pulled the steering wheel violently from side to side as he fought to maintain control in the soft sandy soil while tapping and releasing his brakes just enough to keep from plowing into the oncoming end of a guardrail protecting a steep hillside.

His entire focus was on staying upright and not hitting, or missing, the guardrail. They would roll for sure if he took the hillside on the outside of the rail. He came to a dusty stop just a few feet from the end of the railing. Finally, he looked toward the truck which had almost wrecked him and Missy. It was continuing south and seemed to be gathering speed.

"You son-of-a-bitch," Bert yelled after the driver, though knowing it would go unheard. "Where'd you learn to drive?" Then the next thought hit him, as he gathered his composure and began to calm his breathing. "Was that just an inattentive, reckless driver, or did he try to run me off the road?"

Bert turned to look for Missy and see how she fared during his sudden stop. He was happy to see her unhurt, though looking around wildly and panting nervously from where she had landed against the back of the passenger seat. She sat on her haunches, looking at him as if to say, "what the heck just happened?" Bert leaned toward her and patted her reassuringly, until her whining subsided.

He backed his vehicle from the end of the railing and rolled carefully back onto the interstate. They would proceed on to the Terry Ranch, since it wasn't much farther. They both needed to get out of the car for a few minutes. He didn't speed his usual five miles per hour over the limit, as was his custom. His eyes were on the rearview mirrors, too. He knew he was not going to overtake the offending pickup.

As he and Missy strolled around the nearly empty "cow town" and campgrounds at the Terry Ranch, Bert found himself still shivering from their close call. The more he reviewed the incident in his mind, the more convinced he became that this was not an accident. That driver almost certainly intended to run them off the road. Norah was right, the wolf was onto them. Almost certainly, but no proof!

As they drove back toward Cheyenne, Bert called the Governor. He decided he wouldn't say anything about the incident that just happened. No need to worry this man any more than he already was.

"Good afternoon, Governor, this is Cody calling. Just seeing what's new with you guys, and if you want to go to dessert central for another piece of that great pie?"

"Hi Cody," the Governor answered, "I'd love to go there. We'll need to hurry because I think they close at 2:00 on Sundays. If you want, let's meet at the same gas station near the west place in an hour-and-a-half."

"Fantastic, looking forward to another culinary treat with you." Bert was sincere. "I'll see you at the station."

Since he was almost at their meeting place on his drive back from the Terry Ranch, Bert had time for another short walk with Missy while waiting for the Governor. She would have to wait in the doghouse for a while until he returned. She was used to that, so he knew she'd be fine. It was still about 40 degrees outside, so would be comfy for her in the car.

The Governor took Bert back to Shari's Restaurant, near the Prairie View Golf Course. This place had some great looking and tasting pies. They left their phones in Sam's vehicle, and decided to sit inside near a back corner with a view of the door. "Good stuff," Bert exclaimed, "If I keep eating these great pies with you, I'm gonna have to go on a diet soon." They both laughed as their forks went from pie to mouth in unison. "Anything new, Sir?"

Sam savored and swallowed his bite of pie before he replied. "Yes, maybe, but I'm not convinced. The second interview of Andrew Atkins' roommate brought out the possibility that Andrew had supposedly talked about eloping with Sammie. This Larue character claims that Andrew was infatuated with her and talked about being in love with her on numerous occasions. He says he didn't mention this during the first interview because he didn't want to get Andrew in trouble."

"Oh, good grief," returned Bert, "Do you think there's any truth to that, Sam? What are the cops doing with this revelation? I assume they've gone over their social media."

Sam seemed ticked. "Well, the Laramie police are talking with the Cheyenne guys. Chief Holcomb has assigned three of his top investigators to look into it. I've known Andrew all his life, and I just can't believe that he'd run off with Sammie."

"So, what's going on with Jeremy Holland, now?" asked Bert. "Does Chief Holcomb still think Holland is the perp?"

"Holcomb is still investigating Jeremy and digging into any and everything from his past and record. He still thinks Jeremy had to be involved, regardless of whoever else might be." Sam didn't seem assured. "I'm inclined to agree with you, but I guess we can't be sure yet."

"I suppose the Atkins are upset about this accusation toward their son?" Bert already knew the answer to that.

"Oh, you know that, I'm sure!" Sam agreed. "I met with Jim late this morning and he's very concerned about where his son is. Just as concerned about what I think of the theory. I told him I don't believe it, but the law has to check it out anyway."

"Damn, this is good pie, Sam!" Bert announced. "So, what we have are a host of possibilities, still. Now among them is the possibility that Andrew and Sammie ran off together; eloped essentially. Another possibility is that Andrew was also kidnapped, and his kidnapping may or may not have anything to do with Sammie's. A third possibility is that he's just out in a mountain somewhere out of touch for whatever reason. And, we can't rule out the motives of his roommate, Larue. Is he telling the truth, or making up a story?"

Sam finished his last bite of pie, took a sip of coffee, and took a deep breath. "So, where do you think we go from here, Bert?"

Bert was wondering the same thing. "Good question, boss. First, did Betsy notice anyone or a vehicle near your driveway last Saturday when you were leaving your residence? We didn't rule that possibility out."

"Oh yeah, I almost forgot to tell you." Sam was almost apologetic. "She said she thought she remembered a dark sedan at the end of our driveway, across the street. She isn't a hundred per cent sure, though, because we see vehicles there often. Might have been an earlier memory."

Bert was a little disappointed but not too surprised. "I think it would be tough to know that for certain, but that's at least a definite maybe, then. That's something, because it means our bad guys might have been surveilling you from there. The first compromise could have started there. Sam, would you get me a copy of the interview with Larue, if possible. I want to know more about this guy. Something about this feels suspicious."

Sam nodded in agreement. "I'll talk with Holcomb about that. I don't think it should be a problem for the Governor to get access to that interview. I'll also get someone on the Records Office register first thing in the morning."

Bert had been studying the fifteen to twenty people in the restaurant, and what he could see out the windows. So far, he could not pick up any suspicious activity. "I think we can go for now, Sam, unless you have something else for me. I'm going to shift gears to Andrew for a time. We must know his situation if we're to rule out any of the others. This possibility could trump any other. He could have the means to run away with Sammie. If he also had the motive, then he becomes the number one suspect. Or, the number one diversion from the real motive."

Sam just shook his head in a show of bewilderment. "Bert," he finally said, "My brain is fried trying to figure out any of this. I must trust in you, my friend. Let's go; I need to get back to Betsy." With that, they motioned to pay their bill.

A new waitress had come in and she now seemed to replace their original waitress as she came to their table. Bert couldn't take his eyes off this very pretty woman. Her blonde hair and blue eyes were set off by a forest green blouse, black skirt, and a silver metallic belt. Even in her polished black work shoes, she looked stunning. "I'm taking over as your waitress," she said, "I'm Becky, Becky Moreland; did you enjoy your pie, guys?" She smiled.

"Sure did," piped up Sam, beating Bert to the punch. "Really good, but we have to go now. Nice to meet you Becky. I'm Sam. Do you work here regularly?"

She smiled and replied in a sweet voice, "Yes, I just started working here a week ago, so learning the ropes, but I enjoy working with the public, and we have great food."

Bert now jumped in, "It's nice meeting you, Becky. I'm Cody. Do you always work the day shift? We'll ask for you when we get back here."

"Yes, days and evenings. I'll watch for you two. Let me take care of that check for you." Becky took their money and headed for the cash register.

Sam looked at Bert and laughed. "Well, we needed a break from all the mental confusion, and she is some break. I think you agree, Bert."

Bert felt himself feeling sheepish. This beautiful waitress had completely taken his mind off the case for a minute. "She certainly did take away my mind, Gov. I guess we better get back to work, huh?"

Becky returned with their change, which they both left for her, and with a smile she said good-bye and come-back, and then went off to other customers. Bert and Sam headed for Sam's truck and back to reality.

CHAPTER NINE: A CLOSE CALL

Back at the motel after another good walk on their road, Bert settled down to his laptop. It was time to first check up on the chat coming from the Chief, and his friend Jess. There was nothing new, just a couple of mentions of FP that didn't provide any real answers. Jess seems to have a working relationship with this unknown entity.

Larue Boynton appeared to be very active on social media, as would be expected for a younger, twenty-five-year-old, guy. Bert gathered that Boynton had only been assigned to the Laramie area about six months ago by the large pharmaceutical company for which he was a traveling salesman. He didn't have many local Laramie connections, but instead talked mostly to people back in New Jersey, where he grew up. His mother evidently died about five years earlier, and his father lived and worked in the area around Philadelphia. He was a big executive for some major corporation apparently headquartered there.

Andrew Atkins seemed to have many friends whom he communicated with around Laramie and Wyoming in general. Bert only reviewed Andrew's chat going back a few months, because there was so much of it. However, he saw numerous references to Sammie Patterson, always in a favorable and positive manner. They apparently visited often at the Governor's residence in Cheyenne. He got the sense that Andrew and Sammie were close; however, there was not the feeling of an infatuation or sexual relationship. Of course, if there was a love relationship going on, they would probably be discreet about it, given the situation with their fathers.

Andrew was in love with the country and mountains. He talked a lot about his day trips and longer camping excursions into the mountains. It seemed that Andrew especially liked going into the Snowy Mountains, as the locals liked to call the Medicine Bow Mountain Range. That made sense since it was close to Laramie. The last comment which Bert could find was made on Sunday morning, the day after Sammie disappeared, when Andrew seemed upset by her apparent kidnapping. He made a comment on his Facebook page that he felt like running away to his mountains.

There were not many comments on the media pages of either Jim or Andrea Atkins. Those were entirely asking for any information about the disappearance of first Sammie, and then later their son. Those comments and pleas seemed to be sincere, as best Bert could tell.

He pushed his laptop away and leaned back against the desk. So many possibilities were flooding his mind, that it was increasingly difficult to keep them straight. The sun would be setting in another half hour, so he decided to take Missy out for a quick walk on what was becoming "their" road. It was close to the motel, yet just a sandy country trail between cow pastures, with a few rolling hills to make it interesting. He needed to clear his mind before he came back and tried to analyze where he seemed to be with the case. After that, he looked forward to connecting with Norah once again. He wanted to know if she was coming home on Monday. He hoped she was.

Out in the parking lot, Bert led Missy around their vehicle, urging her to check it out for anything unusual. This time, she alerted on and yapped at the glove he had paid another motel customer five bucks to plant inside his back bumper. Her effort was rewarded with a good chunk of deer jerky. With that training session behind them, he loaded Missy in the back, and they drove to their favorite road and the walk she knew was coming.

It was only a few minutes before the sun would be below the southwestern horizon. Bert walked briskly to keep up with Missy, as she was meandering from fence line to fence line, looking for a scent to investigate. She crossed the right-side fence and was checking out a few gopher mounds along the low hillside about 75 yards away from the road.

Bert saw a vehicle, a pickup it looked like, approaching from the east. When it got to within about 50 yards of his position, the truck suddenly slid to a stop and a young man, maybe a teenager, jumped out of the passenger side door. He was carrying something.

Bert felt his stomach sink as he recognized a rifle in the boy's hands, and saw the kid place it across the hood of the truck, aiming toward Missy. Bert yelled loudly and began running toward the truck, yelling for Missy at the same time. It was too late. He heard the familiar crack of a 22-caliber rifle. As he saw Missy turning toward him, he saw the dust kick up near her feet. The bullet had gone low. He continued running and yelling toward the truck.

The teenager was steadying himself for a second shot, when another boy stopped him, and pointed to Bert. Driving into the setting sun, they had apparently not seen him until now. The lad lowered his gun and stepped back from the truck, facing Bert.

Bert slowed to a walk when within about ten yards of the boys. He yelled breathlessly, "Thank goodness you guys finally saw me. That animal is my companion and tracking animal. She's very valuable to my business."

As Missy approached cautiously and sidled up against Bert's legs, the young shooter looked at her with growing interest. "I'm sorry about that, Mister, we see coyotes all the time out here. Their pelts can bring up to twenty-five or thirty dollars untanned. A hundred or more, tanned. Didn't know she belonged to anyone. Her pelt might fetch a couple hundred."

Bert wasn't angry at the boy. "That's okay, son, all's well that ends well. You had no way of knowing. I was careless to let her stray so far from me. We've been walking out here for several days now and you're the only people we've run into. I thought it was safe to let her roam a little."

All three teenaged boys were out of the truck now, wanting a good look at Missy. He saw the opportunity to educate them about the coywolf. They listened intently as the last rays of the sun disappeared over the western hills. In the fading light, he decided to ask them a couple of quick questions.

"You guys are obviously from around here. If you were going to do some wilderness camping, where would you go? Someplace not too far away."

The driver spoke up right away. "Oh, not even a debate. We'd go to the Snowy's, down near Laramie."

"How would you go, any particular trailhead that you guys use?" Bert asked.

The other passenger now chimed in. "We usually drive to Centennial, then go out to one of the several trailheads that go into the Snowy Range. There's just a couple that you don't use."

Bert felt a nudge. "Why don't you use all the trailheads?"

"Well, I guess a couple aren't really trailheads. We've been told they're entrances to corporate retreats and you can't go far down them anyway. So, we just use the others. You can get to the back country easy enough on those."

"Let me ask you guys something," Bert continued, "If you were trying to just get away for a time into the mountains so nobody would bother you, would you go there?"

"Yup, sure would," chirped the passenger. "You can go deep into the mountains out there, if you want to. We've gone there several times on overnights. It's great!"

Bert needed to get back to the motel. "Thanks, guys, I appreciate the info. I'm really glad you shot low back there, too." He looked the shooter in the eyes and smiled.

The boys were ready to go on, also. They said their good-byes, took a last look at Missy, and headed west, kicking up dust as they sped away. They now had their headlights on.

Bert looked Missy over, just to assure himself that a ricochet hadn't nicked her. Once satisfied that she was okay, they set off on a brisk walk back to the doghouse. It was now too dark for them to be out here on this back road.

* * *

"Good evening, love, how are you doing up in that north country? How's your Mom doing tonight?" Bert was glad to be talking with Norah again. He really missed having her near.

Norah was happy to talk again, too. "Hi, Bert, she and I are doing as well as you could expect. Mom is making remarkable progress, and she went home today. My sister is there and will stay with her for the months it will take to completely rehabilitate Mom. I will be with you by this time tomorrow, love, and I'm very excited about being together again. How are you doing with the case?"

Bert couldn't wait to discuss the case fully with Norah. "Honey, this case has more twists and turns than a politician's budget. I could sure use your inputs, once you're here and read in on the case. I think I'm getting close to something, babe, because some guy ran Missy and me off the road this afternoon. I'm not sure, but it sure seemed intentional. Fortunately, neither of us was hurt, but it scared us."

"Oh my God, Bert, you must be very careful, Honey!" Norah was obviously shaken by his acknowledgment. "I've been seeing visions of you in trouble, Bert; this is a dangerous case. I can feel the danger."

"I'm being careful, Sweetheart," Bert assured her. "As you know, though, there are no guarantees in life. Are you feeling or seeing anything else from here, Norah?"

She was quiet for a good while, thinking and allowing the spirits to come to her. Finally, she spoke. "I'm sensing death, Bert. Someone has died there. This person, a male I think, has disappeared and is dead. People are looking for him, but they don't know where to look. I sense he didn't die alone. Someone was with him when he died."

Bert thought about Andrew, and the allegation that he ran off with Sammie. "Do you think he was killed, or did he die by an accident?"

She replied quickly. "He was killed because of something he knew or did, Bert, something to do with your case."

After they said good night, Bert leaned back in his chair, ran his fingers through Missy's coat, and thought about Sammie. Was she out there in the mountains somewhere, with a boy who loved her like a sister? Or maybe not like a sister? A boy who was somehow killed. But who would have killed him? Sammie? Or are they pawns in a grander scheme?

CHAPTER TEN: MONDAY

By 8:00 Monday morning, October 9th, Bert and Missy had performed another good training session around their SUV, taken their usual sunrise walk, had breakfast, and were ready to begin another day. This day would start with contacting Norah followed by a call to the Governor.

Norah was still coming today, and her mother was continuing to do better than anyone hoped. Bert asked if she had any more visions related to this case.

"Sweetheart," she offered, "I'm very anxious to be with you and help with this case. I've missed you so much." She paused to get control of her emotions. "I sense that you remain in grave danger and someone may still attempt to harm you. I feel that this entity is trying to remove you from this case, Bert, they're afraid of you. They fear what you may discover. Continue to be very careful, my love, I will see you later today. Bye for now."

"I love you and I've missed you tremendously, Norah," Bert replied, "I can't wait to have our team intact, again. I'll see you later. Goodbye for now, Sweetheart."

Bert reflected on Norah's words, before he and Governor Patterson arranged to meet at their "dessert central" location for coffee and breakfast. Missy's check around the vehicle was becoming a bit of a game for her, as he always made sure there was something unusual for her to find. This morning, the keys from a cooperative and curious fellow getting ready to leave the motel were the prize. Missy found the unusual scent on her first pass, and excitedly snarfed down her reward of jerky. Bert scanned the area for any signs of an observer, and after seeing nothing suspicious, they headed for the restaurant.

After meeting up, entering Shari's Restaurant, and sitting down to their food, Governor Sam said he'd already directed his Chief of Staff to have his senior administrative clerk get the register from Records. He expected to have this listing by noon. "I've received a briefing on the second interview with Boynton, but the Chief didn't think it's appropriate to give out the transcript at this stage, even to the Governor. What else do you need, Bert?"

"I'm looking into the politics that might be behind Sammie's disappearance. I'm not sure I buy the claims about Andrew and Sammie. As for the roommate, Larue, I mainly want to know what he claims to know about Andrew's relationship with your daughter. Also, any family members or other connections that Larue may have referenced." Bert felt a growing need to dig into this Larue character.

Sam put aside his food for a minute. "Larue claims that Andrew talked about being in love with Sammie, and how he wished they could just go away together somewhere. Larue's mother is deceased, and he says he isn't close to his father. He states that he's very close to his step-dad."

"Step-father?" Bert asked. "So, the mother was married a second time. Did he list her new married name? Or the name of the stepdad? Any mention of where they work?"

Sam had removed a note pad from his front shirt pocket, thumbed it open, and began to respond to Bert's questions. "Yeah, the mother remarried a guy named Harvey Killebrand. The mom's name was Jill. When she married the stepdad, she began working at the same company where he worked. It's a big corporation headquartered outside Philadelphia. His mom, Jill, died just a couple of years after marrying Killebrand."

"Did this roommate ever get over to visit the Atkins? Just

wondering if they've met him and what they think about him?"

"From what Jim has said, Larue was supposed to meet them for the first time the night that Sammie disappeared. Andrew was going to bring him to their house to meet up for dessert and then go to a late movie. Of course, that didn't happen."

Bert wanted to shift gears, so he didn't tie up Sam too long. He reviewed the list of house bills, identified last Friday, and asked Sam if would support and sign any of them.

Sam snickered. "Son, you sure have a nose for the controversial. All those bills are emotionally charged and hot buttons. The jury is still out on the one about the coal industry regs, but I'm leaning toward signing it. I'm flat not in favor of the wetlands bill; too many restrictions already on agriculture in our state. I will sign all the others. We need to have essential oversight in this state."

"Let me be devil's advocate for a minute." Bert stated. "If you were to resign from your office, the lieutenant governor becomes governor; correct? Does he support the same issues that you do, or would he go against you?"

Sam laughed. "No, he's a free thinker, so he says. He and I often have opposite philosophies when it comes to these things. I believe in hands-off government, generally, but I think some industries need significant oversight by the state. Ag lands, state properties, abortion industries, and so forth need to be strictly controlled, in my opinion. Vandersloff thinks we can trust entities like these to largely self-regulate with only minimal oversight. He would probably veto several of the bills that I would sign."

"Very interesting," Bert interjected. "I wondered about that. Boss, I've probably taken up enough of your time for now. If you could notify me when the Records Office register is ready to review, I'll work out a way to pick it up. By the way, what's the prevailing thinking from the police chief about all this??

"Oh, Chief Holcomb is salivating over the Andrew runaway theory. He sees an opportunity for both his major rivals to go under, I think." Sam chuckled at that; half-jokingly. "Seriously, I think he believes this is a highly probable theory."

Bert sat thoughtfully for a minute. "Well, I can see why it's attractive to the Chief. It does answer a few questions about the logistics of pulling off such an abduction, assuming it was an abduction. Andrew, with Sammie's help, likely had all the means needed to pull this off. Key to the back door. Knowledge of the guard's movements and tendencies. Ability to help her out of the house with a sprained ankle. Maybe she faked the sprain. And so on. There's just one main question."

"Yup, would he do this?" It was obviously on Sam's mind, too. "Would my own daughter do this, willingly? I don't believe either of them would pull such a stunt. Why would they? We've never been in their way of seeing each other."

With that, both men said their so-longs. Bert looked around the restaurant parking area in all directions, for any signs of surveillance. He knew what to look for but didn't see any evidence that he was being watched. As he was entering his car, the phone which had been left inside, was ringing. It was the Governor.

Sam called to tell Bert that he was just informed of a press briefing by the Chief of Police, Holcomb, for noon on the Capitol steps. Sam had no idea what Holcomb was going to talk about with the press. He wanted Bert to be there, as Cody, and see what he could glean from it.

Bert took Missy on a quick walk along their motel road, then headed for the Capitol. It was 11:30 on this Monday, the 9th of October. He felt like things were starting to pick up, and he didn't know yet where they were headed.

* * *

Chief Holcomb was at the top of the Capitol steps, looking regal in his pressed and crisp uniform, as the several dozen reporters and other interested parties milled around below him on the steps. Bert had thrown on his previous disguise and felt confident that nobody there was paying any attention to him. All eyes went to the Chief, as he began to speak.

After a brief introduction to why he was there, the Chief related how his investigation had taken a new turn. They now suspected that the Governor's daughter had run away with the son of a prominent businessman and friend of the Patterson's. He had now assigned a team to investigate this new development. While they were continuing to explore all options and leads, this possibility had the feeling of being "very credible. The Chief promised to keep the press updated as new information became available. He asked for the public's continued help in relaying any tips or information to his team. With that, he ended the briefing without taking any questions.

Bert stayed around for a few minutes, listening to the buzz from the throng of reporters before they raced off to send their stories. It was obvious that the press, in general, was excited by this new development and the possibilities of covering not only a crime, but now a scandal.

As he was entering his car, Bert received a call from the Governor. The register from the Records Division was ready for pickup, if he wanted to swing by the Governor's Residence. Sam would bring it out to the end of the driveway and give it to him. He'd be there at 2:00 sharp. Bert looked at his phone for the time. It was now 12:45. He had fifteen minutes to get there.

* * *

He hadn't eaten since his breakfast that morning with the Gov, so Bert arrived at Shari's Restaurant, records in hand. He would look them over while having lunch. He removed his disguise. Missy would stand guard inside the doghouse, while he was inside.

Becky was working today, and she recognized him as he walked inside. She nodded to a table in the back-left corner, obviously part of her responsibilities. Pleasant as before, she smiled and warmly greeted him, asking how he was doing.

"I'm doing great," Bert answered, "Just needed to get one of your chef salads and look over a few documents. How are you doing today, Becky?"

"Hey, I'm impressed, Cody, that you remembered my name!" She seemed genuinely pleased. "I'll be happy to get you a salad."

It wasn't lost on Bert that she also remembered his code name. He laughed. "Well, can't forget a pretty face like yours. Thanks, I'm going to do some work for a couple of minutes. This seemed like a good place to think."

"What do you do?" She asked. "Must be something pretty important?"

He didn't want to go there. "Well, you know your own work always seems important to you; not necessarily to anyone else. I'm no different than any other businessman who has lunch in here."

Becky took the hint; she seemed to know not to press him on that. "I'll be back in a couple minutes with your lunch, Cody." She didn't buy that he was like any other businessman.

Bert pulled out the Records register while he was waiting. He ignored most of the names and times, until he arrived at the two names just prior to his own, at 3:15, and the three after his name. These were the people who were likely inside the office when he checked in; the people who were able to hear his name.

The first two ahead of him seemed benign. They would have been sitting somewhere out in the offices, by the time he checked in, and probably not likely to have heard his information. One identified himself as a local real estate developer, the other as an engineer for what sounded like a mining support company.

Those in line behind Bert would have been able to hear him provide his basic information to the office clerk, though. The first, a male, gave his name as Harold Johns and his position as chief operations officer, and listed an address of Casper, Wyoming.

"Here's your salad, Cody," Becky was smiling at the table's edge as she placed a large chef salad near his paperwork. "You must be one busy businessman to have to work at the table in here?"

He pushed his papers aside and pulled the salad in their place. "Wow, that's some salad! Thank you, Becky. Yeah, I'm on a short string to get this done. I'm sure you know how that is."

"Yup," she responded with a laugh, "I do know about deadlines. Such as getting a salad to a starving customer."

He laughed back. "Well, not exactly starving, but I am kinda hungry. Have you always worked around here?"

"No, I'm from Billings, Montana, originally. I just moved here about a month ago and landed this job last week. Not my dream job, but it'll have to do for a while." She looked around to see if any other customers needed her attention.

Bert knew she needed to get back to work soon. "What would you rather be doing?"

She looked back at him with those blue eyes. "I've always been interested in investigation and crime solving. I'm trying to get on with one of the firms here in town and have an interview set for next week with one of them. Waiting on others."

He looked at his salad for several seconds, taking in her words. "Tell you what. If you'd like, leave your name and number with me before I go. I know of another company that you might consider down the road if none of those work out."

"Oh, that would be fantastic, Cody. And it might just be the best pickup line I've heard all day, if you're just teasing me." She smiled. "I'll get my info to you when I bring your check. Better get back to work now."

Bert knew his face was probably beet red. Trying not to look too flustered, he smiled back at her. "Well, if I was that smooth as to use that for a pickup line, I guess I'd surprise myself. Just suggesting another possibility for you, maybe down the road." He felt like he was babbling. Did she notice? Probably! Crap!

Becky was silently chuckling to herself as she went back to work with other customers. She knew he was embarrassed and found it cute.

Back to work, thought Bert, as he took a bite of salad and returned to the office register. The second person in line was a female, Jessica Waters. She gave an occupation of research assistant. She was also from Casper. Was that just a coincidence, or did she work with the first guy?

Last was a male, Leonard Wood, from Cheyenne. He listed his occupation as hydrologist. "A water guy," thought Bert. "A water guy could be interested in the wetlands bill, as well as the mining issue." He pondered that as he finished his salad.

"Here's your check, mister businessman." Becky had arrived unnoticed at his table. "I slipped a little something along with it for you." She was having a grand time teasing this man.

Embarrassed again, Bert gave her a twenty for the bill and told her to keep the change. "That can be my finder's fee if my, I mean the other job I was telling you about, works out." He found her note with name and phone number. "Got to get going, Becky, duty calls. Hey, first can I ask you a quick question. Are you familiar with any company called FP? Just curious, since I can't find it."

She answered quickly. "If we were in Billings, I'd say it was Family Planning. I took my oldest niece to the clinic there last year. She needed help, if you know what I mean?"

He wasn't sure what she meant but could guess. "Okay, thanks. I couldn't figure out what it meant around here. Better be going, Becky. See you next time."

* * *

"I think there's a clinic in Wyoming. Casper, I think. I might have that wrong. Anyway, you have a good day, too, Cody. Stay safe. Come back, ya hear." With that, she turned to another customer motioning for his check.

As he walked out to the car, a troubling thought hit him. Was Becky the spy who was helping keep tabs on him? "Crap! I hope not," he said aloud as he opened his door and climbed inside. A few well-placed licks from an excited Missy took that thought away for a few seconds.

Another thought hit him. Could Sammie have been pregnant? If so, would Andrew be the father? Could this Family Planning connection, if it is a connection, not be a coincidence?

Since it would be several more hours before he would get back with Norah, Bert decided to give Missy another good run at the Vedauwoo trail. Like before, there shouldn't be anyone else out there on a chilly, breezy October day. They headed west on I-80.

Bert sat back down at his chosen picnic table, near one of the larger rock formations. He leaned back and looked at the Snowy Range to the south and west across the interstate. Missy was doing her thing around the rocks, whining, yapping, and looking for anything that might be chased. He decided to give her a twenty-minute walk. After that, he was ready to do some thinking.

The Atkins' son, Andrew, had somehow become a pivotal character in this mystery. Bert had the feeling that the roommate, Larue, was somehow connected to this disappearance. But how? He decided to check out Larue's parents more when he got back to Cheyenne. Maybe there's a clue there?

There's something fishy about the Chief of Police. Bert felt he needed to continue looking at the Facebook account. Especially the conversations with that Jess guy.

He also needed to do a follow-up with the security guys. He'd try to make their happy hour group tomorrow and see what the scuttlebutt is all about, now.

"I also need to meet up with the Governor tomorrow morning and see . . . . what the hell!" He looked across the interstate toward the south area of the park. Sitting near a distant table was a lone dog, a Husky. It was on its haunches, and seemed to look at him, then look away to the west. His eyes followed the dog's, and he leaned forward for a better look.

Zing! Splat! Crack! The whine of a bullet as it whizzed by his head was followed immediately by the impact on the stone formation behind him, then by the familiar crack of a distant high-powered rifle. Bert instinctively fell forward off the bench and dove to the ground. He laid very still, his eyes searching to the south. The Husky was running west toward the man of previous encounters. They both turned and disappeared into the nearby trees.

Bert continued to lie still. Maybe the shooter would think he'd hit him? Missy was running frantically toward her master from her gopher hunt several hundred feet away.

For several minutes, Bert didn't move. If the shooter was still watching him through a scope, maybe they'd think he was fatally hit? Missy was whining and licking his face feverishly. He resisted the urge to react to her long tongue. She didn't understand his need to be unresponsive.

Finally, after nearly ten minutes in his prone position, Bert decided to risk moving. He slowly raised his head and searched the area from where the shot came, to the south or southwest. It came from the direction of the dog and its owner. Did the guy shoot, or was he with the one who did? Nothing! Nobody was in sight, and no sounds. Whoever shot at him must have disappeared into the wooded hills to the south. Now Bert had to wonder if this was a stray bullet from a hunter's rifle. It was hunting season, and such things were known to happen occasionally. Just last season, a man was killed on his front porch by a stray hunter's round.

Bert stood up quickly and using jerky movements to the right and left, he ran toward the car, jinking as they used to say in the military flying business. Evasive and erratic movements to throw off the targeting of enemy fire. He got to the near side of his vehicle and hunkered down with Missy excitedly at his side.

Then he noticed her acting strangely, whining next to him but going to the rear of their vehicle and yapping. Bert stayed low as he peered around the back of the doghouse. Missy seemed to be interested in something at the back bumper. Bert crawled toward her and reached inside the bumper. There it was, the answer to how they knew he was at this location.

He pried the magnetic tracking device from the bumper. It was one of those Radio Shack looking trackers; inexpensive but effective. Somebody had to have placed it there today, since Missy checked out the car this morning at the motel. Where, though? Shari's Restaurant? Where Becky Moreland worked? "Oh my God," he said aloud. "Is she involved in this?" Something inside him deflated. This was a thought he didn't want to entertain, but he couldn't afford not to.

Bert placed the tracking device on a nearby rock. It would possibly deceive the shooter into thinking the car hadn't moved. He hastily let Missy into the cargo area and jumped behind the wheel. They sped toward Cheyenne; toward Norah, and news she would not want to hear. Finally, though, she was back on the team.

CHAPTER ELEVEN: NORAH'S BACK

"I'm so glad to have you back here, Sweetheart!" Bert said emphatically and sincerely to Norah as they sat near one another on his motel bed. "I can't tell you how much I've wanted to bring you up to speed on this case."

"Oh, darling, you don't know how much I've missed being with you," she said softly, "and helping you with this case, our case."

Bert moved to the desk chair, leaned back with his stocking feet on the end of the bed, and proceeded to tell Norah all about their case. He was very excited to have his spirit love and partner back with him every day. There was one more event he wasn't anxious to tell her about.

After learning of the close call rifle shot, Norah was alarmed. "Sweetheart, I saw that in a vision, and I still see you beyond the end of a gun. You're still in danger, Honey. Death isn't done here. I keep seeing the wolf and he isn't chasing the fox now. I just see it coming toward me, toward us. He's after us, really you, Honey."

Bert reflected on her words for a minute. "Yeah, Honey, I know you're right. So now that you know about our case, baby, are you getting anything else?"

She leaned forward on the bed, her red hair divine on her shoulders, and her small bare feet crossed in front of her. Her eyes were closed, as she looked and listened inside her mind. Finally, she opened her eyes and looked at Bert. "Hun, I still get glimpses of that number 104. I still have no idea what it means. Got to mean something, though. Something else is very troubling to me, Bert."

He leaned forward, listening intently. "What's that, baby?"

She pulled her feet in and crossed her legs, leaning toward him. "Hun, I'm sensing not just death as I've said, but I'm sensing a bunch of death. Not like before, the times I've told you about. This is different. I sense death but have no perception of who's died. It's all fuzzy, and it feels like many have died or will die. It's a frightening feeling, Honey."

Bert took his feet off the bed and sat forward in the chair. "Oh my God, that's a chilling sensation, Norah. Will this case erupt into a blood bath, at some point?"

"I don't know, Bert. But it's one of the more unsettling half-visions I've ever had. It feels like it's somehow connected to our case, though."

He could feel her confusion. "I see why you're upset, Norah. We'll try to figure it out, hun. Anything else?" He could sense that she had more to tell.

"I'm picking up on fear, Bert, a lot of fear. Not just from one person. It feels like these people are afraid for their lives. It feels like they're captives, missing in some way. It's as if they're sending out radio waves, and I'm pulling in one fragment of those waves. They're desperate, Honey. We may be their only hope of returning from the missing."

Bert Lynnes leaned back in his chair again, resting his head against the top headrest, closing his eyes. Were there more people missing than just Sammie and Andrew? Who died? Especially, he wondered, when and where will a significant loss of life occur? Would this rescue require a full-scale shootout?

He opened his eyes and looked at Norah, who had moved alongside Missy, on the floor, close to the canine's furry back but not touching it. Missy wasn't looking at Norah, but Bert could tell she sensed Norah's presence. Her body language spoke volumes, as she stretched, yawned, opened her eyes partially, and then slowly closed them. Her soft whine sealed the deal.

Then a memory began to gnaw at him. Where had he seen the number 104? Somewhere just recently. He began to thumb through his notes, until it hit him. The list of upcoming legislation that would be in front of the Governor, included issue 104, a bill to regulate the state coal industry. Could this be the 104 which Norah was seeing? While this issue would have some controversies, was it all that critical; so critical that it was worth risking prison time? Bert decided he'd have to ask the Governor more about it.

He thought about something else and checked his notes. Yes, Jim Atkins had a business related to the coal industry. Could this be something that Jim and his friend, Sam, might be at odds about?

His gaze went back to his sweet Norah and he saw that she was resting quietly on the rug next to Missy. They had always been best buds, so Bert decided not to disturb her as he quietly got ready for bed. As he slid under the covers and lay on his side looking at his wife, he couldn't help but mouth the words of one of his favorite love songs: "For You," by John Denver. He quietly sang the first few words, "Just to look in your eyes again, just to lay in your arms, just to be the first one, always there for you. . . . ." He drifted off into sleep.

*　*　*

Morning came early on this Tuesday, October 10th. Norah accompanied Bert and Missy on their pre-sunrise walk down their nearby favorite dirt road. She loved the red glow in the eastern sky as they strolled easily along in the chill of a 30-degree morning. Missy's coat was getting increasingly thick and luxurious. It would glisten with its reddish tint in the first rays of the sun.

They returned to the motel just before the other guests began to leave. Bert slipped a $5 to one of the men if he would plant something anywhere under his car, for Missy's later training. Norah was pleased that Bert was taking this extra precaution and teaching Missy a new skill.

Back in the room, they began to discuss Andrew and his relationship to Sammie. Bert asked but Norah had no perceptions of a love relationship between them. "Just not perceiving anything about that," she said. "However, I sense fear from them, Bert. Something isn't right. I guess that goes without saying for an abduction, huh."

Bert nodded in agreement. "Well, if you're sensing fear from both, that likely means they were both abducted. They probably didn't just run away together. We need to look for two abductees, not for two runaways."

"Norah," he went on, "Do you sense anything about a policeman?"

She again leaned back toward the headboard and quietly reflected on his question. "I'm not getting a good feeling, Bert. Not sure how to explain it. Usually I feel a sense of safety, security, with a cop. I'm not getting that feeling now. Does that make any sense to you?"

"Yeah, it does," he replied. "There's a cop, a Chief of Police here in Cheyenne, who might have reason to see Governor Patterson quit. All political."

She digested his words for a few seconds. "Would he kidnap the Governor's daughter just to try to make Patterson quit?"

"Don't know, Sweetheart. That's one of the many questions. All I can say now is that it's possible, it seems." Bert rocked back in the chair with his fingers pressed together at his chin. "This guy is known to have political ambitions."

Norah sat forward again. "The boy who is also missing, Andrew I think you said, what is his connection to drugs, you know, pharmaceuticals? I'm seeing pill bottles along with sensing fear."

Bert processed her words for a second before answering. "The only connection I know of is his roommate; a young guy named Larue. He reportedly works as a pharmacy rep for some company. So, you're seeing a connection with pharmacy drugs in some way?"

"Yes, darling," she answered quickly, "I just don't know how it connects."

He leaned forward with elbows on his knees and cupping his chin in his hands, thinking. Finally, he looked up at Norah. "I think we need to focus on Andrew's roommate, Larue. There are now several signs which hint toward him, including yours. I want to meet up with the security guards later this afternoon and see what they know about this. They've been open with me. After that, let's start tomorrow looking into this Larue and his background. There's something about him that keeps pulling me there, too. How about a drive and give Missy a good walk? Then I'll check in with the Governor before going to meet the security guys."

Bert led Missy and Norah out to the doghouse and noted with satisfaction that Missy readily took his command to search the vehicle. This was the first time that he did not have to actively lead her search, and she was very excited about finding the old glove planted earlier by another guest. After giving it a good shaking, she sat proudly with her ears perked up, expecting to be rewarded with a piece of deer jerky.

Bert decided it would be interesting to drive a few miles east of Cheyenne on Interstate 80 and visit the unusual mechanical creations at the Mel Gould property of Buryville. This self-made inventor had crafted numerous metal sculptures and weird vehicles. A wind machine, aptly named the "wind thing," powered the lights at the property. Bert would give Missy a walk around the property and marvel for a few minutes at the creativeness of this man.

The few minutes turned into nearly an hour, captivated by the magical sculptures and underground workshop, before Bert returned Missy to their vehicle. Norah had chosen to stay in the car.

On the way back to Cheyenne, Bert called Governor Patterson to ask if there were any new developments. Governor Sam said he'd like to meet for a quick piece of pie at dessert central in two hours. Bert realized he had just enough time to drop Norah and Missy back at the motel, so they could relax there for a bit. After that, he headed for Shari's restaurant. He needed to be there within an hour. He couldn't help but wonder if Becky Moreland would be working. He also wondered if she was on the side of the wolf.

It was about 1:30 in the afternoon, when the Governor pulled up to Shari's. He said a quick hello to Bert, and they went inside. Sure enough, Becky was working. She saw them come in and motioned toward a table in the left rear of the dining room, where she obviously would serve them. They went there and sat down.

She looked stunning as ever. "What can I get you gentlemen today? Are you having a late lunch or is this another of those business meetings?"

Sam was all business this time. "I just want a piece of peach pie, Becky. Kinda on a tight schedule today. How about you, Burrr.... Cody? I'm buying." Almost screwed that up, he was thinking to himself.

Bert was quick to respond. "Oh, thanks Sam, I'll have a piece of that peach pie, also, Becky. We're both on tight schedules this afternoon." Both he and Sam followed her with their eyes as she went after their pie. Bert turned to Sam and they both smiled. "Hard not to notice a looker like her," Bert offered.

Sam nodded in agreement. "Bert, I'm increasingly concerned about the situation with Andrew. Despite the runaway theory, which is gaining traction with the law guys, Jim and I both agree that our kids just wouldn't do that. When we look at the timeline of events the night Sammie disappeared, some things don't add up."

"What's that?" Bert asked. "I'm with you there. I can't help but feel there's more to that story."

Sam continued. "For one thing, that Saturday was going to be the night that Andrew was going to bring Larue to their house and introduce him to Jim and Andrea. They were planning on going there early and waiting for his folks to get home from our event. When Andrea called to tell her son they'd be late because of Sammie's accident, she had to leave a message because he didn't answer. Not sure why? When Andrea called the second time, Andrew answered, and she told him about being late. They never got to meet Larue. He had left when they got home; only Andrew was there. The next day, Andrew disappears. All we have to base anything on is Larue's statement about them being in love and running away. I don't trust him, Bert. Something just smells fishy."

"I know, it smells fishy to me, Sam. I want to do some checking into Larue's family connections. There might be something there that can shed some light on this."

"Pie anyone?" Becky said enthusiastically, as she returned to their table. She smiled at them both as she placed a big piece of peach pie in front of them, then turned without another word and went on to other customers. She knew they were engaged in an important talk. No time to interrupt.

They ate several bites of their pie before Sam finally spoke. "Yeah, I agree that you need to focus on Larue for a while. Unless we can discredit this runaway story, everything else seems to be taking the back burner. If these kids did run off together, then Jim and I want to know that, too."

Bert thought for the couple of minutes it took for him to finish off this tasty pie. "Sam, my psychic is back on-board full time. She sees some signs which seem to point to Larue. I'm going to follow up on them. I'll let you know what I find out."

Sam started to speak but stopped as Becky returned with their checks. "Back for the money, honeys," she said laughingly. "I can handle these if you like, as I know you gents are busy today."

Bert chuckled as he returned her smile. "Thanks, Becky. I appreciate your recognizing that we needed room to talk. We've got some big decisions to weigh. Got a lot on our plates. Have you had your interview yet with that investigation company?"

"Well, Cody, just keep some of our pie on your plate now and then. I'm always glad to see you two in here. No, I have an interview tomorrow morning. Wish me luck; I'm very nervous." With that, she took their money to the register, as Bert and Sam proceeded to leave. Bert took one more glance at her shapely figure as he went out the door. Back to work.

As they approached their vehicles, Bert paused to ask Sam if he could get the campaign finance records of Police Chief Holcomb.

"There might be something there; who knows," he said.

The Governor nodded in agreement as he entered his truck and drove away. Bert decided to put Missy on the leash and have her do a security check on his vehicle. She had been acting a little anxious when he opened the door. She alerted on the back bumper. Bert cautiously and as discreetly as possible knelt beside the rear bumper and felt along the inside. Finally, he found it; another tracking device placed this time near the top curve of the inside bumper. Whoever put it there apparently did so while they were inside Shari's. He decided to leave it there. Maybe it would be a good idea for them to track his movement to the Outlaw Saloon?

As he departed Shari's parking, he carefully looked for the telltale signs of surveillance. Nothing! "Why at Shari's and why when Becky is working?" he wondered. "Connection, or coincidence?"

CHAPTER TWELVE: CLOSING IN

Bert pulled into parking at the Outlaw Saloon, between two pickup trucks. It was nearly 4:15. The security guys would show in the next half hour or so if they were going there. He let Missy out on her leash for a minute, walking around his vehicle. When discreetly hidden by the surrounding vehicles, he quickly knelt, removed the magnetic tracking device, and just as quickly placed it inside the back bumper of an adjacent truck. Whoever was following the device was in for a surprise. He put Missy back in the car with windows well down for ventilation, quickly put on his mustache and military jacket, and sauntered inside the saloon.

The one older guard, Larry, was at the same table, and recognized Bert. He motioned for him to come over. They exchanged greetings and small talk, ordered a pitcher of lager beer, and then Bert gradually maneuvered the talk where he wanted it to go. "How's that young guard holding up? The one who might be getting setup or framed," he said.

Larry seemed almost anxious to talk. "That kid is nervous as hell, Cody. He's still working at the same place, but his every move is being watched. Some of the heat came off him this past few days, though."

"Why's that?" Bert asked.

"They're now thinking the missing girl might have run off with a love interest; another young college kid from Laramie."

"You don't say? That's an interesting change of events. Do you think there's any truth to that?" Bert was genuinely interested.

Larry wasn't shy about discussing it. "It's hard to say. From what I'm hearing through the grapevine, they're basing it on the kid's roommate, some guy who works as a pill salesman. Apparently, this guy alleges that."

"What's this guy's other connections?" Bert asked.

Larry shook his head. "The scuttlebutt is that they're not looking into this guy's history much. They only care about confirming the runaway allegation. Interviewing other students, checking the kid's social media, you know, that kind of stuff. The Chiefs involved seem hell bent on proving this angle. They have his and the girl's pictures on all the news. Listed as runaway lovers."

"Crap, I have to get the news more," Bert thought to himself. Then he asked, "Larry, do you recognize the initials FP? I heard that the other day, but don't know what it references."

Larry thought about the question for a minute. "I'm guessing that it may refer to that Family Planning company, which has a secondary headquarters outside of Casper."

"What's the deal with them?" Bert wanted to know.

Larry again shook his head. "Well, there's the public perception and the actual reality, from what little I know. The business is portrayed as a women's health and family planning champion. If you dig into it a bit, it sounds like the real business is providing abortions. One of my friend's daughter got knocked up about a year ago. She was only fifteen. They took her to Casper for what turned out to be an abortion at the clinic there.

"Oh, I see," Bert was surprised. "Is this a local company, or national?"

"I'm guessing it's national," said Larry. "I think there's one in Billings, too."

Bert already knew about the one in Billings. "That's interesting,

Larry. Well, brother, I must be going, but it was good talking with you again. We'll need to have a beer here again."

They said their good-byes and Bert returned to his vehicle. As he entered, he noted with satisfaction that the adjoining pickups were still there. Whoever was monitoring his movements would be misled a bit. He chuckled about that but felt the unease that comes from knowing you're being surveilled.

Driving back to the motel, he took several unusual turns, looking for signs of a following vehicle. He didn't see anything. Apparently, the bad guys were still relying on their tracking devices to watch his movements. They obviously know his vehicle, though, and that concerned him. After the apparent assassination attempt, what else might they try?

Back at the motel, Bert discussed the situation with Norah. "Sweetheart," he asked, "Are you getting any more insights into this?"

She leaned forward from the bed headboard; legs crossed, and with hands clasped in front of her and chin resting on her thumbs. This was one of her favorite thinking positions. Finally, she looked up at him. "I'm feeling a sense of dread still, and despair, but also a feeling of betrayal, Bert. It's a feeling of hopelessness, and darkness. Like being in a dark tunnel or a cave. It's an awful feeling that makes me feel almost nauseous."

"Who do you think you're channeling, Honey?" he asked.

"It feels like a young person, Sweetheart. I'm not sure but it feels like a male, a younger male, maybe. Andrew maybe?"

Bert thought for a minute. "Do you pick up anything else about this young male?"

"Two things are coming to me, Bert," she replied. "I'm seeing some kind of a sign, kinda rectangular, you know. It seems worn, like it's been in the weather a long time. I think it was black at one time, but is now sorta grey-like, from weathering maybe. I'm seeing white letters on it, or at least they used to be white. She went on, haltingly. I think they are K, E, F maybe, I or T, then what seems to be D or maybe O, something, and maybe another I? It's so worn that it's hard to make out, and I feel like I'm seeing it in a dark environment, maybe at night. It feels like I'm seeing from a dim light, like a weak flashlight. After that, I feel that sense of dread and like I'm in a cave." She leaned back with a pained look.

Bert knew she was living what she was seeing, and it affected her. She was on the verge of crying. He sat back and thought about her vision and started to write down the letters. He studied them for a few minutes. Then a picture began to take place in his mind. "Sweetheart, could that old worn sign have said 'keep out' in capital letters?"

She thought about his words for a second. "Yeah, I guess so, Honey; I think so. That seems to fit, worn as it is. So, keep out of what?"

"I guess that's the real question, isn't it?" Bert replied. "If your vision of a dark, cave-like structure, maybe a prison, is on point, then maybe this sign is near the front of it. If that's the case, then this must be an old building or such. Do you think this could be where Andrew, and maybe Sammie, is being held?"

"It feels like that, Bert, maybe?" She wasn't sure. "It does all seem to tie together."

Bert wanted to try to summarize what they had. "So, Honey, it seems like you're sensing that both Andrew and Sammie are in fear and seem to be captives, perhaps together. You sense betrayal, which could apply to either or both of those kids, if they were in fact taken hostage. Someone obviously betrayed Sammie and might also have betrayed Andrew. Could that someone be his roommate, Larue?"

"Didn't you say he was a pharmaceutical rep or salesman?" Norah asked. "I did have a vision that had something to do with pills."

"Yes, that's right, baby. That seems to tie Larue to Andrew's disappearance. We need to find out more about this guy. I'm going to get online in a minute. First, I want to find a rental car that will work for us and have it delivered near here. The bad guys know our vehicle now. Maybe we can buy some time with a rental. Then I'm going to see what else I can find out by digging deeper into Mr. Boynton's family connections."

Norah nodded her agreement and she turned her attention to Missy, who was stretched out on the floor in front of the bathroom. She moved to Missy's side and quietly and ever so softly stroked her head. Though she barely moved a hair, Missy stirred, stretched, yawned, and arched her back, as she sensed Norah's touch. Bert knew that their souls were communicating. It was a beautiful thing to watch.

He lined up a Ford extended cab pickup, one of the few with darkly tinted windows and room in the back for Missy. The dealer would deliver it to the motel in the morning around 8. Their car will just remain parked in the parking lot.

Then he began the online dig into Larue Boynton's background and family. Investment into several online people search programs was going to pay off with this guy. Boynton began to emerge after two hours of research.

Larue's real father died when Larue was only seven. Three years later, his mother, Jill, remarried a guy named Harvey Killebrand. It appeared that Killebrand and his stepson became quite close. When Larue was sixteen, he started working part time at the stepfather's company, while his mother began working there as an executive secretary. A few years later, she came down with breast cancer and subsequently died when Larue was about nineteen. At the age of twenty-one, Larue landed a job as a pharmaceutical representative and salesman for a leading company. This company seems to be closely aligned with Killebrand's company: FamPlan corporation, headquartered in Philadelphia.

Looking into FamPlan, Bert began to see a troubling coincidence, or connection, to his case. FamPlan is the parent corporation for its most profitable subsidiary, Family Planning. The same Family Planning with clinics in Billings, Montana, and Casper, Wyoming. Bert finally found an excellent article about this company.

An investigative reporter in, of all places, Lincoln, Nebraska, had chosen to do an expose' on this company and the abortion industry. Bert learned that this is a huge money-making business, nationwide, and FamPlan is one of the biggest. The reporter discovered that less than 10 percent of the company business comes from actual family planning. Nearly 90 percent comes from the business of providing abortion related counseling, the medical procedures, and, to the reporter's and Bert's surprise, the harvesting and selling of fetal tissue. The multi-billion-dollar yearly enterprise is among the Fortune 500 list of the largest companies in America. The Family Planning clinics are in all 50 US states, and they are where the business and customers come together.

Then a potential bombshell emerged from this reporter's investigation, one which has been almost entirely ignored by the major news outlets. The expose' discussed the landmark bill being fleshed out in the Wyoming legislature, and which would likely make it to the Governor by early next year. This bill, if it passed and became law in Wyoming, would be the first of its kind and precedent-setting. The proposed restrictions, should they be enacted in all 50 states, could cost the entire abortion industry billions of dollars. The industry, led by FamPlan, was gearing up to wage a major fight against the Wyoming bill.

Bert leaned back and let out a big sigh. "Was this the wolf in Norah's visions? Is FamPlan behind Sammie's kidnapping to remove Sam Patterson from office before the bill reaches his desk? The Lieutenant Governor seems to oppose the bill. If he became interim Governor, he would probably veto it. Larue worked with his mother and stepfather in the corporate offices of FamPlan, before he became a pharmaceutical rep. Was he planted as such in Laramie. Was it a coincidence, or design, that he offered Andrew Atkins a shared apartment? Andrew's father, a known candidate to replace Sam Patterson as Governor, shares Patterson's views. He would almost certainly sign the abortion bill, if he were to replace Patterson. Is Larue behind the disappearance of Andrew as a trump card to keep Atkins away from the Governor's office? Was Andrew becoming too aware of something fishy? Bert had to assume that this could be true.

He turned to Norah, who had returned to her place on the bed, watching him work. "Norah, I need to ask you something about that troubling vision or feeling you had of many deaths. What does that look like to your mind, Honey?"

She thought a minute. "Sweetheart, the best I can describe it is if you're looking through a frame covered by wax paper, and there is unbelievable carnage on the other side. You mostly just sense it without making out any details. Why are you asking, Bert?"

"Honey, I have to ask you this. Could this relate to aborted fetuses? Perhaps from one or maybe many clinics which specialize in abortions? Are you sensing the deaths of those who were too young to have developed personalities?"

Norah pulled her knees up toward her chest, wrapped her arms around her legs, and laid her head on her knees, eyes closed. Finally, she raised her head and looked at her husband, her eyes moist with tears. "Yes, Bert, that could be what I'm sensing. Do you think that abortions are somehow involved in this case?"

Bert proceeded to tell her what he had learned about FamPlan and Family Planning, and the possible connection to the bill in committee within the Wyoming legislature. "Our case may be connected to the abortion industry, and in particular to the FamPlan system. I'm not absolutely sure, but the signs are pointing that direction."

She sat quietly, reflecting on his words. "So, what do we do next to prove this, Honey?"

"There's something I want to ask Governor Patterson in the morning. And I want to do more research into the local Family Planning clinic; maybe the national organization. There's something here that we're missing. I'm not sure what it is, but I'm sensing that. Right now," he said, "I think we should turn in. Tomorrow might be a big day. I love you, Sweetheart!"

"I love you, too, Bert, and I'm glad we can share this business together. I like working with you. I know we're going to solve this case and get Sammie back. I feel that."

Missy left her place in front of the bathroom and moved in front of the window, her favorite spot in motels. She lowered her head and tail and did four quick circular turns, clearing her bedding place for the night. She lay down in a curl, her head resting on her front legs, tail curled around her belly, and closed her eyes. Secure at last!

"Good night, Captain Sparrow," Norah stated in a guttural voice. "See you at the gangplank at sunrise."

"Aye, Matey," he replied. "Next stop, Davie Jones' locker." They laughed quietly as they drifted toward sleep.

CHAPTER THIRTEEN: IN THE CROSS HAIRS

Clouds had rolled in during the night, bringing a gloomy cold to the eastern Wyoming landscape around Cheyenne. Bert's morning outing with Missy was reduced to about fifteen minutes, as the twenty-degree temperature seemed like ten with the fifteen miles per hour breeze. Sunrise was only represented by the lightening of the eastern horizon and cloud cover. It was Wednesday, October 11th, 2017, marking the one-week anniversary of his involvement in the search for Sammie Patterson. Back at the room, Bert would call her Dad, Sam Patterson.

First order after breakfast, though, was the delivery of the rental truck. Bert disguised his look, went for a walk down the street a couple blocks, and met up with the truck delivery. He didn't want to be seen at the motel getting a different vehicle. He would get Missy and Norah at the end door of the motel later, rather than the usual front door. He parked near that end exit and entered the motel.

"Good morning, again, my love," he said to Norah as he entered their room. She was sitting on the floor by the front window, with Missy. "We have the new rental pickup, a black Ford extended cab. With a little discretion, hopefully we can throw off the surveillance for a day or two."

She nodded her agreement, and resumed her communion with Missy, who lay stretched out beside the bed, snoozing after her morning walk.

Bert called Governor Patterson. He asked about how the family was holding up, then if he was able to get the campaign finance records of Chief Holcomb.

"Yes, sure did," replied Patterson. "I can get the listing to you this morning, if you'd care for a piece of pie at Dessert Central in two hours?"

Bert agreed to the meeting and made one more request. "Sam, could you also get something else that might be interesting, please? I think it could be helpful if we can review the resumes' and job applications for your administrative staff. Especially those hired within the past three years, basically during your time in office."

"That should be no problem, Cody; I'll see if my admin chief can get that together right quick and I'll bring with me in a few. See you there."

Bert hung up the call and turned to Norah. "Sweetheart, I'm going to meet with the Governor about getting what might be some key documents. If you notice me gaining weight, blame it on the Gov. He's making me eat a lot of pie since I've been here." They both laughed, as Bert donned his old military jacket and cap and headed out the door. Missy would stay in the room with Norah. Bert placed the "Do Not Disturb" sign on the outer door as he left.

He exited the end door of the motel, entered the Ford pickup, and drove to Shari's Restaurant, making several unexpected turns as he traveled, just in case someone was trying to follow. He saw no signs of a surveillance vehicle and arrived nearly a half hour early at the restaurant. He would go inside and get a jump on a piece of pie until the Gov arrived.

Bert was well into his piece of apricot pie, when Sam Patterson entered and sat down at the table. "Darn good choice there, Cody," Sam noted, "I haven't had apricot pie in a coon's age. Think I'll get one, also." He waved to the waitress.

As they sat savoring their pie, Sam passed a large envelope to

Bert. "This has both things you asked for, Cody. The campaign finance record is just for the last election which Holcomb was in. My staff's resumes' go back only three years. There are only four people, one woman and three men. All are administrative help."

As Bert reluctantly took his last bite of pie, a tiny half-bite he was saving to the last, he opened the envelope and took out Holcomb's finance record. There were literally hundreds of reportable small donations to his campaign in 2014. Bert glossed over those. He was looking for large contributions. Thankfully, the record was arranged from the smallest to the largest. He finally found what he was looking for by the time Sam had finished his pie and was on his last few sips of coffee.

"Are you finding anything?" Sam asked.

"Maybe, Sam. A company named FamPlan donated $5000 to Holcomb's campaign. Family Planning, in Casper, made a similar donation of $4000. I recognize two private individual donations of $2000 each, from a Harold Johns and a Jessie Palmer."

Sam did the math in his head. "That's about $13,000, if my math is correct. Are they tied together in some way, Cody?"

"Yes, Sam, they are tied together, I think. There is evidence that all are related to the major entity, a national company named FamPlan, headquartered near Philadelphia. Right now, this might be only circumstantial. It may not mean anything. But it might mean something, too." He removed the job applications of the four administrative people.

It didn't take long for Bert's scan of each application to produce the result he was looking for. One male, hired two years earlier, listed a three-year employment at Family Planning in Casper, prior to seeking employment by the Wyoming Governor's administrative office. Bert felt a chill run down his back.

"Sam," he asked, "How well do you know this guy, Steven Swaney?"

Sam was quick to reply. "Not real well other than at work. He seems like a nice guy, about thirty years old, I'd guess, and he does his job well. Never had any problems with him. In fact, he's been so reliable that he's been entrusted to oversee our security program."

Bert thought about that for a couple of minutes as he sipped his last bit of coffee, purposely stalling his answer. "Would Swaney have access to your keys, security cameras, and the like?"

"Yes, he would be able to access those things, since he's responsible for overseeing all that." Now Governor Patterson sat rigidly upright and looked Bert in the eyes. "Are you thinking that he and the others are all tied to this Family Planning business, and they might have something to do with this?" His voice became more intense with a hint of growing anger.

"That's what I'm suspecting, Sam. However, right now, my friend, I can't prove anything. It's critical that we do nothing to alarm anyone. Be aware but keep this information to yourself for now. Keep your eyes and ears open, boss, but don't tip your hand. If I'm right about this, your daughter's in a life-threatening situation. We can't blow our chances of finding her by broadcasting suspicions."

Sam leaned back in his chair and took a deep breath, exhaling slowly. He knew he had to control his frustrations and fear if he was to get his daughter back. "Okay, Cody, I know you're right. What do you need me to be doing?"

"Sam, I think right now you should mostly focus on your family and office and leave this case to us. Keep an eye on the investigation into the runaway lover theory for us, though. My focus is trying to figure out where your daughter might be hidden. To do that, I have to know who's behind this."

Sam seemed more at ease now. "Cody, I know your team will do everything possible to find Sammie. I must get back to the office, like you said, so gotta go. How about we plan for lunch around 1:00 tomorrow afternoon at Shari's? We'll update everything then, unless something significant comes up."

Bert agreed, and they paid their bills and departed their respective ways. Again, he varied his route back to the motel with several unusual turns, looking for any clue of surveillance. Nothing! Back at the motel, he parked the Ford near the end door, but entered by way of the central front lobby.

"Hello, my dear wife," he said as he entered the motel room. Norah and Missy were sitting near the AC unit in front of the window.

"Howdy, partner, how's Kemo Sabe doing?" She snickered.

He laughed back, "Doing heap big fine, Tonto, got um good stuff this morning. Now must walk trail into cyberspace and find bad guy."

She became serious now. "I'm guessing that you found out some things which make our path look a little clearer?"

Bert gave her a quick rundown on the evolving picture as he perceived it. He pointed out how several individual trails all seemed to have a connection to FamPlan, and all converge with the here and now. "Now we have to figure out if any of this can lead us to Sammie, and maybe Andrew."

"I don't know how this helps, Honey," she said, "But I'm feeling drawn to mountains and forests, and I keep seeing that number 104. I still don't know what it means. It feels like it's painted on something."

Bert contemplated her words momentarily. "Do you still feel like these kids are alive? Are you being pulled by either of them?"

Norah took an inward look, seeking answers, with her eyes closed. "Yes, Bert, I'm feeling the tug of a young woman in trouble, and with great fear. She's somehow connected to that old Keep Out sign. And to death, at least one death."

He was troubled by her perceptions. "Do you know, or can you get a sense of who may have died, Sweetheart?"

"No, only death, possibly more than one. Somehow, Bert, possibly two deaths have occurred in connection with Sammie's abduction. Maybe more."

Bert thought about that for a minute. Still without any idea of who she could be channeling, he turned his attention to his laptop and the internet for answers.

He started to pull bits and pieces of information from digging into the online trails. Looking back in time at Holcomb's message traffic with the mysterious Jess Palm, he made note of a reference to a "get together next weekend." This was in early September of this year. In a conversation that Larue Boynton was having with his stepdad, Harvey Killebrand, there was also a mention of "see you soon" made in late July. A bit later they again mentioned getting together at "the cow town." Bert turned his attention to the websites of FamPlan and their Family Planning office in Casper.

FamPlan had an extensive website, much of it devoted to their support of women, women's needs, and issues. He eventually came to a company events link. One event was listed generically, without specific date or details, and just referenced the yearly "Wyoming Retreat" in September.

On the Casper Family Planning website, he found more references to the "upcoming retreat, and later in mid-September to the great time the middle and upper managers had at "Cow Town," this year. "Is this the same Cow Town that Larue and his step-father had mentioned?" Bert wondered. He continued looking deeper into the website.

In an area devoted to their managers, he found other references to Cow Town. One caught his attention. This one paragraph talked briefly about the annual retreat on September 8th through 10th at "Cow Town, outside Centennial." It talked about how this was a great opportunity for advancement in the company, because high level leadership from "corporate" would be there. Bert leaned back in his chair, his mind putting together an emerging picture.

The key players, to include Police Chief Holcomb and Larue Boynton, apparently met in early September with the leadership from the headquarters of FamPlan. This took place in a corporate retreat somewhere near the Wyoming town of Centennial. Centennial is located about an hour drive to the west of Laramie and is a gateway to the Snowy Mountain Range. Sammie Patterson disappeared three weeks after the retreat. Andrew Atkins shared an apartment with Larue, in Laramie, and disappeared the following day. The boys who shot at Missy said they camped all over the Snowy Range, and there are trailheads marked as something like corporate property. Bert drew a deep breath and exhaled slowly. Had he discovered the wolf and its den?

"Norah, my love," he said with an air of excitement in his voice. "I'm going to take Missy out for another walk and let my mind digest what I've been finding out online. While I'm gone, could you focus in the area of Centennial. I think we may find our answers, and possibly Sammie, there."

"Yes, love," she willingly agreed. "I'll see if I can direct my feelings and thoughts in that direction. I don't often try to influence what comes to me, but I'll try to make this an exception and see what happens. I'll see you in a few. Enjoy the walk; I know Missy will!"

Bert put Missy in the back-seat area of the extended cab, entered the cab, closed the door, and looked in his rearview mirror. Startled, he just sat unmoving. On the far side of the parking area, another pickup had backed up and was preparing to leave, sitting without moving for just a minute. Looking over the back of the truck was the greying haired man, wearing a brown leather jacket. He seemed to be looking at Bert's vehicle. It almost seemed like he was looking at him in the rearview mirror; a chill ran down Bert's spine. Bert shifted slightly to change his view in the mirror. A Siberian Husky was standing just to the rear of the truck, a few feet from the man. It also seemed to be looking in Bert's direction. Bert felt himself nearly freeze to his steering wheel with a sense of fear bordering on terror. He forced his eyes off the mirror and onto the steering column and the key in his shaking hand. He started his vehicle, and then looked back in the mirror. The truck behind him had departed, and along with it the man and dog were nowhere to be seen.

Bert just sat in his Ford rental, not moving. They knew his every move, it seemed, and now they obviously know what he's driving. What else do they know? He reached his still trembling hand back and stroked Missy's head. She seemed to sense that something was wrong and had reared onto the seat back, her head near his. Her soft fur and gentle whine helped calm Bert's nerves. He backed from parking and proceeded toward their walking trail.

The five-minute drive and the two miles walk were cathartic, and Bert's mind slowly settled down. The overcast was giving way to the partly cloudy skies of midday, and they welcomed the occasional warmth of the sun as it peeked through the holes. Halfway down their trail, Missy encountered a badger about fifty feet to the north of the road, where it had been digging. He stopped to watch them, wondering if this was going to end well. Badgers are nothing to mess with.

Missy circled the badger, about five feet from it. Her back was arched into a hump, and she walked almost stiff legged, her teeth on display. Her wild instincts were obviously coming to the surface, and Bert found himself feeling a slight sense of fear at his own companion's fierce behavior. She was showing a side of herself that he had only seen once, in Nebraska, some weeks earlier. Her injury didn't seem to hinder her at all. He let out a whistle and called her by name.

Not too distracted by the badger to ignore her alpha male, Missy slowly backed away from the badger, which was hunkered down in its defensive posture. Her body language gave way to that of a companion animal of the human she trusted. She slowly turned away from her adversary and began her coyote lope back to Bert. Conflict averted, this time.

He resumed the walk, his mind replaying the earlier encounter at the motel. It was an uneasy feeling to know that the bad guys know where he and Norah are staying and what they are driving. They have already probably tried to stop him twice now. What else are they willing to try? Also, what's the role of that guy with the dog? Is he a scout, a lookout, a PI, a hit man?

His attention turned back to Missy again. She was at the right fence line, in hot pursuit of vermin, probably a ground squirrel.

It was giving her a merry chase, ducking around the fence posts and back and forth through the fence, slowing her down. At one point, it ran up a post to the top, but had to retreat to the ground as she literally jumped over the fence, snapping at the prey as she passed. A couple seconds later, it found sanctuary down a burrow. Missy frantically dug at the mound and surrounding soil, dirt flying twenty feet behind her. After about twenty seconds of attempted excavation of her snack, she slowly gave up and walked away, hesitating every few feet to look back. Maybe the little morsel would show itself again. It didn't!

The remainder of the walk was uneventful, except for the couple of red-tail hawks circling overhead, scouring the ground for a meal. They arrived at the pickup and drove back to the motel. Once inside, he gave Norah the rundown on Missy's adventures, then chatted with her about the probable need to meet with the Gov and tell him about the convergence of the trails and see what he might know about Centennial. Norah agreed and said she'd be happy to stay in the room with Missy.

Governor Patterson, who always seemed to both love and need the pie and lunch breaks, was quick to agree. He said he'd prefer to get lunch at Dessert Central, since it was crowding 1:00 in the afternoon. Then he jokingly said the scenery was usually pretty good there, too. They both laughed in agreement. Both relished any break from the mental demands of this case and trying to find Sammie.

Bert reached Shari's Restaurant first, and found a table in the back corner, an area he knew was usually covered by Becky. There was no sign of her, though. He felt a twinge of sadness at the thought that she might not be there today. Sam Patterson soon arrived and strode up to the table and sat down. They shook hands and ordered lunch from a young waitress. Bert asked her if she knew where Becky was today. She nodded and said at a job interview, but she'll be back at her restaurant job at 2:00.

"So, Cody, are there any new developments on your end?" Sam knew there were.

"Yes, Sam, as you suspect, there are things I've been pursuing which seem to be coming together. Like we discussed the last time we met, I've been following up on leads among key players, and those leads are pointing to possible, maybe even probable, involvement by FamPlan Corporation and its leadership. This seems to have something to do with an annual retreat somewhere near Centennial. The recent retreat took place in early September, about three weeks before Sammie disappeared."

"So, your suspicions are being confirmed then?" Sam inquired.

Bert didn't want to overplay the suspicions. "I don't want to mislead you, Sam. My suspicions seem to be supported by what I'm finding. However, suspicions aren't facts. I don't think we have enough to take it to the DA. There's still the question of where your daughter might be held. If we play either a wrong hand or the right hand too soon, it could decrease the chances of bringing her home safely. That's our primary objective; get your daughter home alive."

Sam was perplexed. "Despite the fact that signs are pointing to this FamPlan company and their retreat, you're saying we shouldn't make a move on it?"

"I understand your desire to get after someone, Sam," Bert countered. "However, the bad guys, whoever they are, know about me and they've tried at least once or twice to take me out of this case, physically. If they're willing to do that to me, think what they'll do with Sammie if they feel the heat. You hired me because you didn't know if you could trust those around you. It's looking like you were wise, because there's growing reason to suspect some of those you'd normally rely upon. You still can't fully trust the team around you, Sam. If we make a move too soon, there's a good chance someone will betray you. That could put Sammie in more danger."

Sam leaned back and inhaled deeply to calm his nerves, something he had to do a lot lately. "Yeah, I know you're right Bert, oh shoot, I mean Cody." He looked around to see if anyone caught his slip. Nobody seemed to be paying any attention to them. "So, what do we need to do next?"

Bert had been thinking about this question, too. "My friend, I do think we have sufficient reason to doubt certain people around you. For one, Chief Holcomb. I think you need to be very guarded about anything you share with him about what you know or suspect. Also, your administrative guy, Swaney, is suspect. I believe you should take steps to quietly limit or remove any responsibilities he has regarding your security. Don't trust any information to him until this is resolved. Better safe than sorry. My team will continue to seek information which might lead us to Sammie."

Sam leaned forward, arms on the table, looking Bert in the eye. "Okay, Cody, I trust your team. We'll do this, and . . .. Hi Becky, how are you today?"

Bert turned to see Becky Moreland almost to their table, looking stunning as always.

She smiled widely and seemed to practically glow. "I'm doing great! I just had an interview with the PI company I mentioned, and it felt good. I think I did well and feel like they're going to offer me the job. I should find out tomorrow. How are you two gents today?"

Bert was quick to respond. "That's fantastic, Becky! If you get hired, will you team up with an experienced person for a while, until you learn the ropes?" He knew that's what should happen.

"Yes, I understand that I'd be paired up with another woman who's been with the company for several years. We'd probably work together for up to a year, depending on the cases that come to us. I'm really excited about the possibility and can't wait to find out if I got the job. I've dreamed of being a PI for years."

Sam spoke up. "Good luck to you, Becky, I'm sure we both will be rooting for you. Although I, at least, will miss seeing you in here. You're like a breath of fresh air."

Ah, that's so sweet of you to say that, Sam. I'll miss you guys too, you're probably my favorite customers." She almost whispered the last sentence so other customers wouldn't hear. "Maybe we can just meet for lunch now and then and catch up on the goings on?"

Bert added his encouragement. "That would be great, Becky, and I also wish you good luck. Be sure to let us know if you get hired. Hopefully, I'll still be here in Cheyenne to cheer for you."

She was motioned by another customer and had to leave their table, but with a big smile and a nod. Bert had to wonder if it was her beauty, personality, or infectious smile that made her so likeable. Most likely it was all three, he thought.

Nagging inside him, though, was the knowledge that he seemed to be frequently compromised when he came to her place of work.

Bert and Sam wrapped up their talk, paid the young waitress, returned to their vehicles, and went their respective directions. Once again, Bert varied his route back to his motel, ever alert for signs of a following vehicle. He saw none. Back at the motel, after giving the rundown to Norah about his meeting with Sam, he decided to do a quick training session with Missy. To his surprise, she took an immediate interest in the doghouse, which had remained parked since getting the rental pickup. She seemed to alert on the drivers' side door. He got on hands and knees and peered under the vehicle.

At first, he didn't see anything unusual and he brought out a small LED penlight for a better look. He was shocked to locate a round disk, about ten inches in diameter and one inch thick, attached, apparently magnetically, to the chassis next to the driveshaft. He felt the hair on his neck freeze and a sense of fear wash over him. He backed from under the vehicle, quickly but carefully, his mind racing.

"Now what," he said aloud to Missy. Then to himself, he wondered what to do next. If he called in the cops, he ran the risk of tipping off a key suspect, the Chief. He couldn't leave it there to threaten other motel guests, though. If the bomb, assuming that's what it is, is rigged to go off with the vehicle's movement, then it will be okay for a while. If it's on a timer, that's a different story. He needed someone with experience to look at it and tell him how to deal with it as safely as possible. Doug Blanchard and the other security guys jumped into his mind. He went into their motel room to advise Norah, then with his usual disguise on, he and Missy headed for the state capitol.

It didn't take long to locate Doug, who oversaw security inside the main door. When Bert asked Doug for a couple minutes of time privately, Doug quickly arranged with another guard to stand in for him a few minutes. He sensed that Bert needed serious help.

As soon as they reached one of the benches outside on the Capitol grounds, the total absence of visitors on this chilly October day made no issue of a private conversation. Bert explained the situation, and for the first time told Doug of his real undercover work, without getting into details. Doug knew not to ask questions, and he quickly knew the man to call. Another former military member of his team had been a bomb disposal guy on active duty. Doug knew they could trust this man's opinion. Isaac was his name, and since he happened to be off duty, he answered Doug on the second ring. After only two minutes explanation, Isaac said he was on his way to the motel just as soon as he rounded up his equipment. Doug had to return to his security work but arranged for Bert to meet up with Isaac at the motel.

Bert reached the motel first, parked well away from the end door, then briefed Norah. She wasn't surprised by this attempt to silence the investigation. "Just today, Honey, I've been sensing our Dodge going out of control while on the road. It felt like the steering wheel went crazy, and then we jerked around and rolled over the side of the road. Not really a vision as much as a feeling. A bad feeling."

"Oh no, Sweetheart, what an awful feeling that must be. You're apparently right on point, though; our wolf is looking for ways to take us out of this case. I didn't tell you, but I saw the mystery man and his dog earlier today on the other side of the parking lot. Like before, they're just watching me, and then they leave. This guy seems to like taunting me; maybe he's hoping to intimidate me into leaving. I hate to say it, but it's working! I sure feel a bit intimidated by him. Especially when I find a bomb under our car after seeing them."

She moved to the picture window and looked outside, in thought. "I'm not picking up anything on this man and his dog,

Honey. Nothing. When I try to focus on Centennial, as you asked, I do feel something. Right now, it's hard to explain. I guess I could say it's a pull, like I'm drawn there. If Sammie is near there, I think maybe I'm being drawn to her fear. I think that's where she is, Bert."

Bert saw a pickup enter the parking area and park a row behind their Dodge. He presumed the driver was Isaac. Advising Norah, he went outside to meet this fellow soldier.

After the initial greeting and handshake, Bert told Isaac all he could about the device under their car. They both assessed the parking area. There were only a couple of other cars there currently, and no guests. They agreed that Bert would go inside and advise the front desk he was having some car trouble and a mechanic would be working on it. This should dispense with any suspicions from the lone clerk, while Isaac did what he had to do.

Isaac didn't bother with protective gear. He knew if this device exploded, he would be dead, with or without it. He had to get up close to make his best estimate as to how it functioned. For fifteen minutes, flashlight, voltmeter, and a small probe in hand, Isaac studied the bomb from every angle. Finally, he crawled out from under the SUV.

"Bert, I'm 99 percent certain that this IED is home-made by an educated amateur. Also, that it isn't on a timer. It appears to be triggered by the vehicle speed. I'm guessing that it's roughly set at a higher speed, such as when on the interstate. That makes sense, since it appears to be rigged to explode outwardly more than up. It would take out the vehicle drive system, wheel tie rods, and so forth. Between the high speed and expected loss of steering, this was intended to cause a serious wreck."

Bert digested Isaac's words. "Oh boy, so they wanted us to be in a major crash the next time we drove somewhere. Can this be parked here safely, then? I don't want to put any motel guests at risk."

"Yeah, I think you can safely leave the car parked here for now. Just make sure nobody can drive it. Take the keys for sure and disable it under the hood. I'll help with that, if you want?"

Bert wasn't a mechanic. "Yes, please, I'd appreciate your help. Once this case is wrapped up, I'll report this to the authorities for proper disposal." Isaac agreed as he proceeded to disable the vehicle. Ten minutes later, he departed, and Bert started back toward the motel end door. The sun was sinking below the western horizon, giving a brilliant red glow to the scattered clouds. Time for a quick walk with Missy.

Following a quick hello with Norah, Bert led Missy outside, and they proceeded down the road in the direction of their dirt trail. They probably wouldn't get to much of the trail tonight. They had only gone a few hundred yards when Missy's cousins took up a chorus in the distant hills. Yapping excitedly, they seemed to be taking roll call, reporting their individual presence to the darkening sky. Bert stopped and listened, one of his favorite communions with the natural world. Missy was also taking it in, sitting on her haunches, head cocked from side to side and facing the chatter. Her soft whining told Bert that something primeval was trying to awaken inside her domesticated mind. She stood up and did a couple of circular turns on the leash, whimpering. Bert knew that despite her devotion to her alpha male and female, there was still something missing from her wild heart. He knew that feeling, himself. A yearning that tugs at the soul.

He knelt beside Missy and caressed her head and stroked the hair along her back, purposely trying to connect his soul with her's. He could sense her quiet longing for the wild and her kind. It was a deep longing that he also felt at times like this. There is an endless ache within one's heart when a deep-seated need cannot be fulfilled. For him. Missy could possibly yet attain her yearnings. He knew that if she chose to leave, she could.

The walk was a short one this night. It was dark when he and Missy arrived back to the motel. Once inside their room, Bert fed Missy as he told Norah about the day's events. She was beautiful as she stood near the window, quietly listening to his observations. When he told her about the coyotes, she looked lovingly at Missy, her eyes moist. She also understood such yearning. It tugged at her soul, too. She turned to her husband. "I love you, Bert; always have; always will. You're the Captain of my ship. I want to hold you so much."

He felt an overpowering urge to hug her. "I've loved you since the first time I met you, Norah. Always have; always will. You're the wind in my sails."

"Tomorrow, Sweetheart, our ship sails to Centennial. We're going to find Sammie Patterson."

CHAPTER FOURTEEN: RETREAT

Bert, Norah, and Missy were in the Ford pickup and headed for the interstate before dawn. He wanted to be away from the motel in the darkness before sunrise, to minimize the risk of being noticed and followed. Missy's quick run to the perimeter of the parking area for overnight relief would be rewarded by a longer stop at the Vedauwoo park. Their Dodge remained parked where they left it. So far, so good! They headed west on I-80 toward Laramie.

The sun was up when Bert pulled into the empty parking area on the north side of the interstate at Vedauwoo Park. Missy was pacing and whining with anticipation to be out of the truck. The second he opened the passenger door, she leapt out, and spun in circles of excitement, and then crouched down, waiting for her master to join in a chase. Bert pretended a charge after her, and that was all she needed. She took off into the stacks of stones, running full speed with tail flying behind. Vermin had better head for cover.

Norah laughed at Missy's antics. "That is one happy coyote." She said. "It's always nice to watch her having fun when she can get out and run. It makes up for the guilt I sometimes feel at keeping her away from her kind. I know she must feel that lonely pull of the wild, sometimes."

Bert understood and agreed. "Yeah, Honey, I know exactly how you feel. When she sits and listens to her cousins yapping, sometimes in the evenings, I sense a longing in her that touches my heart. I must remember that she would have died as a pup if not for us. We gave her a life, a good life; in exchange for giving up what she may have had in the wild, probably death."

"I know that's right, Bert. We must stay focused on that and realize that she will always feel that pull. Speaking of feeling a pull, Honey, I'm having a weird feeling right now. I sense something sinister and it's pulling my thoughts to the west, toward Laramie.

"What's she doing over there, Bert?"

Bert turned slightly to look at Missy, where she had emerged from behind a rock formation, about twenty yards behind them. She was standing rock still, staring past them toward the interstate. Her eyes were fixed on something, her ears were erect; her tail was low to the ground. He turned to his left and followed her gaze. On the westbound highway, a dirty brown pickup was passing the exit, headed toward Laramie. He couldn't see who was in the cab, but in the back stood a grey and white dog. It seemed to be returning Missy's stare, before turning to place the wind in its face. Bert stared, unblinking, as the truck disappeared down the interstate. A chill floated down his back, causing him to shiver. Was that the truck that ran them off the road? Was that a Siberian Husky in the back? The Siberian Husky?

"Honey, what are you feeling and are you sensing or seeing anything?" He asked Norah.

"Like I said, hun, I'm feeling a sense of dread, like a pull toward doom. This feeling just came over me the past few minutes. There is something sinister to the west of us, Bert, and I'm seeing deep forest and rocks. Something bad has or will happen, and we're headed toward it. I'm scared, Bert! You're in danger."

Bert nodded his understanding. "Do you get any sense from a man and dog, or just a dog?"

"No, Honey," I get nothing about a dog. Just the feeling I told you about." She seemed resolute.

"We need to get going, Norah, whatever's out there, it's concealing

Sammie, maybe Andrew, too." He whistled for Missy, loaded her, and they exited the park and headed west on I-80.

Thirty minutes later, Bert exited the interstate in Laramie, and checked his phone's mapping application for the directions to Centennial and the Snowy Mountain Range. A light snow was beginning to fall on this grey, overcast day. They arrived at the intersection of highways 130 and 230, both headed into the mountains. Bert looked at Norah. "Where do you think, Darling? Right to Centennial or the mountains to the south of it?"

She didn't hesitate. "Go to the right, Honey, toward Centennial. I'm feeling the pull from that direction. I'm also sensing that number 104 occasionally, too. I'll know what it means when I see it. I'm connecting with Sammie's fear, I believe. She's somewhere that direction."

Bert took the north fork, highway 130, and piloted the pickup west on this state road. He knew not to question Norah, when she connected with a victim. It also fit with what he had learned about the Cow Town Retreat.

As they proceeded through the town of Centennial, Bert made a mental note about the Old Corral Hotel and Steakhouse, the Antlers restaurant, and the Beartree Tavern. When this was over, he wanted to see this little mountain community and enjoy a drink and a good meal. For now, though, it was all business as they headed west of town, still on highway 130, also known as the Snowy Mountain Scenic Byway. Several inquiries in town about the location of the Cow Town Retreat had been met with an uncertain collaboration of "maybe out 130 a ways." This was obviously a secretive facility and the locals knew little or nothing about it.

Several miles passed along this Snowy Mountain Road, with no sign of a retreat. A sense of frustration and doubt began to creep into Bert's mind, exacerbated by a slight increase in the snowfall. Here in the mountains, it wouldn't take a lot to force them to abandon their search. Suddenly Norah almost shouted.

"Bert, stop! Something's not right."

He pulled into a driveway and stopped. "What is it, Dear? What's not right?"

She was animated. "We're passing her somehow. I'm feeling the pull to the left of the road. We have to back up."

Bert backed past the mailbox and onto the road and drove back in the opposite direction. In a couple hundred yards, a private road cut off to the south of highway 130, at that point. A sign said that the ski area was ahead, indicating on west on highway 130. They pulled onto the well-maintained gravel road about a hundred yards, where a heavy metal gate and a "Private Property; Keep Out" sign stopped them. He parked in the turn-around area by the gate. Apparently, they weren't the first to be at this point.

"Now what?" Bert said aloud to nobody in particular. "We can't go any further. What's your spirit telling us to do, Sweetheart?"

Norah was sitting silently, head slightly forward, and eyes closed. Finally, she opened her eyes and looked at her husband. "She's somewhere up that road, Honey. I'm sure of it. I feel her pulling me."

Bert was still, quietly reflecting on her words. The light snow was still falling gently with virtually no wind. The less-than-an-inch buildup gave no hint on any recent traffic through the gate. Norah was being pulled up into the forest on this winding trail. They needed to know what was up there. If this is it, then he had to go.

He turned to Norah. "Hun, I'm taking Missy and walking up this road. We have to know if this is the place. Hopefully her nose can help us confirm it." He brought out Sammie's hairbrush, enclosed in a plastic bag. It would provide the scent for Missy. Instinctively, he drew his 40 caliber Ruger semi-auto and chambered a round, and then flicked on the safety before holstering it. He knew the first round was a hollow point, a bullet designed for the sole purpose of killing. There were cougars in these woods, too.

Norah nodded her agreement. Her eyes glistened as she looked at him. "I know that, Bert. Be very careful. I don't want anything to happen to you; I love you." She sat back to begin her vigil; a vigil wrought with concern and unease. She watched as her husband and their tracker moved around the gate and started up the road.

Bert and Missy had only gone about a hundred yards up the winding road, through the heavy forest, when they arrived at the real gate. This eight-foot-high gate, with similar chain link fence going both directions from it, was topped with barbed wire on outward-leaning barriers. The gate was hinged with an automatic opening device which could apparently be opened remotely from somewhere inside the enclosure. A twelve-foot tall log entrance spanned the gate, with a large sign across the top. White letters on a dark green background welcomed guests to "Cow Town." This was indeed the retreat that Bert was looking for!

As Bert studied the gate and strained to see anything up the road, which continued to wind up the hillside through a heavy stand of trees, he noticed the security camera. Without looking straight at it, he walked to a far side of the gate area. In his peripheral vision, he saw the camera slowly turn to follow his movement. There are security personnel inside this compound, he thought to himself. They know that he's there. Now what?

He moved about fifty feet back down the road and called for Missy. With his back to the gate and camera, he knelt and rubbed her all over and gave her a big hug, hiding her features from the camera as much as possible. Then he rolled a snowball and heaved it down the road away from the entrance, knowing she'd chase after it. He stood up and trotted down the winding trail with her until he knew he was out of sight of the gate's camera. Maybe they'd consider him just a guy out for a walk with his canine.

When they were about halfway back to Norah and the vehicle, Bert stopped to look at Missy. She was standing very still, head and ears erect, her eyes fixated on something out in the woods on the north side of the road. He couldn't see anything in the dense tree cover. A low guttural growl emanated from her throat. The show of her teeth told him she perceived a possible threat. He quickened the pace back to their pickup.

At the pickup, Bert opened the driver's door and explained to Norah what they had encountered. "We've got to find an alternate way into that retreat, Honey, there's no way we can bypass the inside gate and fence. Maybe there's a game trail down where we turned around on that north side. I think Missy and I will see if we can find any way to get us close enough to look inside. We'll just keep the pickup locked. If anyone does check it out, they will likely think a guy and a dog came out here for a walk. We've left plenty of tracks for them.

He put Missy on the leash while they walked back up the road. Something was tickling at his mind, but he couldn't make it out. Something had crossed his consciousness when they turned around to go back to the entrance to the retreat. Then his attention diverted from that question to something else. Near where they'd turned around, on the opposite side of the road, the side the retreat was on, he noticed someone walking into the woods. Was there some kind of trail there that might get him and Missy close to the retreat?

When they approached the place where he'd seen the walker, sure enough, a faint game trail soon became clear to a trained eye. It disappeared up into the low mountain hills and forest. The snow had lessened to just a few flakes, and the inch or so on the ground wasn't a big problem, other than making hidden rocks slick. He let Missy off the leash as they began working their way up the narrow path of lightly trampled vegetation. The patches of snow had a few deer and rabbit tracks. Bert was pleased, because the game trail seemed to be going in the direction of the retreat. Undoubtedly, it would lead to an upper level area of vegetation and natural shelter for bedding down during the days. He easily traversed the trail, while Missy roamed and explored the woods just a hundred feet or so around him.

After nearly a half hour on the slow, winding path, Bert caught his first glimpse of the guy he'd seen walking. It appeared that this guy was well ahead of him but also following the same game trail. He wondered what would bring him all the way up here. This wasn't exactly an easy hike, though he'd been on a lot that were much harder.

About ten minutes later, he discovered one reason the first guy might be up here, he seemed to be walking a dog. Bert just caught a glimpse of the animal as it roamed around its master, just as Missy was doing. With the increasingly rugged terrain, heavy forest, and light snow, he couldn't tell much about either of them. An uncomfortable feeling began to come over Bert. He is following a man and a dog. Could this be the same mysterious man and dog that were shadowing him throughout this case? Were they ahead of him, watching him? Did they know or suspect that he would take this path? An uneasy sense of vulnerability began to set in.

He felt for his pistol and rechecked the safety.

About forty-five minutes later, Bert and Missy arrived near the apex of the game trail and it began to dissipate near the top of the low mountain. He found a clear area atop a cluster of boulders and surveyed the area around him. The paper map he had brought along now became his guide as he compared the terrain around him to that on the map. After several minutes, he determined that he must be about a half mile just north of the likely location of Cow Town. Now, how to get there?

The terrain to the south was quite rugged. A steep canyon with even a few short cliffs stood in his way. The tree cover was giving way to rocky and rough terrain, before it rejoined the heavier forest at a lower elevation. Hopefully, the retreat was hidden in that portion of the forest. Bert assessed the sky. As the clouds continued to thin, he knew he only had about four more hours before darkness would overtake the day. He had to pick a way and get down there. No time to waste.

As Bert pondered the options, he noticed Missy acting strangely. She was looking toward the upper side of the canyon, whining. He looked where she seemed to be looking. Part of the way down that side, an animal was moving in the direction they wanted to go. Bert couldn't tell what it was, but there did seem to be a game trail there. He headed for the right side of the canyon.

Fifteen minutes later, he knew they'd made the right decision. The game trail was easy to follow, and they made good time and were nearly past the canyon. The trail seemed to fork as they neared the more level terrain and started into the woods. The left fork appeared to make a slow descent probably toward the area where Norah was waiting. The one to the right seemed more likely to take them to the main retreat. He started down the right fork, but suddenly stopped. Up ahead, just about to enter the deeper forest, was the walker dude. He seemed to be sauntering at an easy pace. If he was just out for a stroll, then maybe that wasn't the way to go, Bert reasoned. It must not go near the retreat. However, the left fork looked like it descended back in the direction of the gates and his pickup. That's not where he wanted to go. Missy made up his mind.

She had been whining and acting nervously for a couple of minutes. Bert couldn't figure out why. Uncharacteristically, she suddenly bolted off the game trails and straight for the forest in between. Bert recognized her aggressor posture, and as he looked in her direction of travel, he caught just a glimpse of a grey and white animal, probably a dog. It disappeared into the woods, as Missy was in hot pursuit. Bert followed her as safely as he could, trying not to stumble over hidden rocks or tree limbs. Was that the Siberian Husky? It had the coloring, but he didn't get a good enough look to determine more. Why wasn't it with the owner? The master seemed to be several hundred yards to the right. Bert broke into a cautious run. He had to catch up with Missy without calling for her. If the other man wasn't aware of them, he didn't want to make him so.

Entering the heavier forest, Bert whistled for Missy, continuing to run in her last direction of travel. After several minutes of increasingly frantic search for her, he stopped and listened for sounds other than his own labored breathing. At first, he heard nothing, but then the faint sounds of something drew him forward.

Cautiously, and with pistol drawn, Bert moved toward the sounds. Eventually, Missy came into view. She was climbing around on a large pile of stones, which were partially covered by brush and limbs. Apparently, she had gotten sidetracked by some vermin in there. "C'mon, Missy," he spoke quietly, "We've got work to do, girl." She somewhat reluctantly gave up her search of the rocks, though she kept looking back for a minute or two as Bert kept motioning for her to follow him.

They walked slowly down the wooded slope, as occasional rays of sun slipped through the pine needles. The clouds and snow had given way to clearing skies and afternoon sunshine. Then he saw it.

Sitting on the other side of a barbed wire fence sat a Husky, looking at them. It was only about a hundred feet from them. Was it the same animal he'd been seeing with that stalker guy? It might be. If it is, that means the owner is somewhere nearby, too. "Perhaps with a rifle aimed at me, at this instant." Bert thought to himself. "Have I been lured out here with the intention of killing me in this forest?" For sure, it would be hard to find his body out here. He took shelter against a large pine tree, and carefully surveyed the surroundings.

The fence?

Bert studied the fence. It appeared to be a professionally installed barb wire fence, which ran right and left from 50 feet in front of where he stood. Likely, it was an extension of the fencing from the gate of Cow Town. Cow Town must be on the other side. He looked beyond the fence into what must be the retreat grounds. At first, he didn't see anything. However, as his eyes adjusted to the dimmer light within the tall pine forest, he saw that the dog was trotting into the compound.

He watched this animal with curiosity as it moved gracefully down the moderate slope, until it stopped in front of an older looking structure. The Husky seemed to be sniffing at a door for a few seconds, and then it trotted around the far side of what looked to be an earth-bermed building. It disappeared for about ten seconds, and then reappeared. Now it was running back up the slope to the north of where Bert stood, fixated on this beautiful animal. It seemed to be running toward something, or someone.

Bert turned his gaze in the direction the animal was running. About a hundred or more yards from him, and on this outer side of the fence, a greying haired white man was standing. He was looking toward his dog and waving for it to come to him. As the animal approached him, he turned and seemed to look at Bert. Then he began hurriedly scrambling to get back up toward the canyon they had traversed. Bert watched them for about fifteen seconds, until they disappeared. "Why is this guy running away?" he whispered under his breath. "If he's hunting me, he's found me. What's he scared of? What's down there?"

Turning back to focus on the old building, Bert had an idea. "Missy," he said in a hushed tone, "Come here, girl." He dug into the small day pack he had brought, until he found what he was looking for.

Presenting Sammie Patterson's hairbrush to Missy, he gave her the order she loved. "Missy, find." She smelled the brush for several seconds, and then turned away from him. She took a few slow, deliberate steps, turning her head from side to side, reading the air. A soft breeze was wafting into their faces, traveling up through the trees from down the slope. Ever so slowly, Missy proceeded down the slope toward the retreat, through the barb wire fence, and toward the old building. Her pace quickened as she got nearer to it. Bert followed her, climbing through the wire fence. He was now guilty of trespassing on private property.

Using trees and bushes to mask his presence as much as possible,

Bert cautiously closed the distance on the building. He noted a foot path leading from the door, winding down through the trees toward the newer buildings of the retreat, barely visible through the underbrush and tree cover. A lone light radiated from inside one of the smaller buildings. The facility was at least a couple hundred yards down the gentle slope from where he and Missy now crouched in front of the door. This old building, which appeared to be an outdated and abandoned wine cellar, was essentially invisible to anyone at the retreat. Above the weathered door, Bert's eyes fixated on a well-worn sign. In barely perceptible letters were the words, "KEEP OUT."

His eyes lowered to Missy. She was sitting in front of the door, whining very softly, the position she took when she found what she was searching for. Bert had to take several deep breaths, trying to calm his racing heart, which he was sure could be heard halfway down to the lodge. He tapped the butt of his pistol against the door; three taps, a pause, and then three more. Only silence.

He tapped three more times, this time a little harder and louder. He waited. Ten seconds ticked by. Then thirty seconds passed. Just as he was beginning to question Missy's skill, suddenly a tap could be distinctively heard from within the cellar. Three taps; then silence. Bert leaned against the door and whispered as strongly as he thought would carry beyond the door. "Sammie, are you in there?"

Five seconds passed. Then he heard the soft voice of a female. "Yes, I'm Sammie. Who are you?"

"My name is Bert Lynnes," he said. "Your dad hired me to find you."

For a few seconds he heard her sobbing. Then she replied in a broken voice, "Andrew Atkins is also here. Can you get us out of this place?"

"I'm working on that. For now, both of you just be as quiet as possible. We don't want any attention from below." He rummaged through his bag for the few tools he always carried. It would take several minutes, but he could remove the locked hasp from the door jamb with a hex-head screwdriver. He knelt and began the task.

Five minutes later, Bert carefully opened the door, allowing daylight to penetrate the darkened interior. Only one small light fixture was illuminated on the far wall. He was surprised that the two young hostages didn't come running out. Surprise turned to anger when he realized that both these kids were tethered to a D-ring in the concrete floor by a very strong leather strap, attached around their waists.

There was no time for introductions or explanations. He had to get them out of here. His sharp hunting knife quickly severed the straps. Both Sammie and Andrew stepped cautiously out into the first freedom in days. "Follow me," he ordered. "Stay exactly behind me; stay close and be very quiet." Pistol in hand, he began to lead them back the way he had come. Missy had instantly attached herself to Sammie, and she stayed next to the girl.

It only took a few steps for Bert to be reminded that Sammie had a sprained ankle that was not fully healed. She was using Andrew as an occasional crutch when she favored her ankle. They were holding hands and seemed very much like a big brother and little sister. He helped them through the barb wire fence, and they began the slow trek up the slope above the canyon.

Once they were well past the fence and on the desired path, Bert turned to study the retreat area while waiting for Andrew and Sammie to catch up. Missy was clinging excitedly to first his and then to Sammie's side. She knew something was up and she took an instant protective attraction to Sammie. Down in Cow Town, Bert was dismayed to see glimpses of lights through the trees. As he focused on the area around the old cellar, he saw a lone guy, presumably a security guard, walking up the path toward it. He appeared to be carrying meals for the hostages. He would be at the prison's open door in a couple of minutes. Bert motioned for his young charges to hurry and stay right behind him. He continued to lead them toward the upper edge of the canyon, and hopefully soon out of sight of the guard.

They were almost out of sight, when Bert heard the faint yell from the guard, and saw him facing up the slope toward them. He then heard the imperceptible, excited chatter as the guard apparently called over a hand-held radio to others down below. Bert told Andrew to help Sammie hurry, and to tell him if he needed help. He hustled, himself, to pick the easiest path along the upper canyon. He caught glimpses of the guard as he climbed through the fence and was running after them. "We have to hurry, guys, they're coming after us!"

As Bert's small group of refugees fled along the upper area of the canyon, which dropped off to their right, he knew the first guard was closing on them and had already reached the canyon trail. He was less than a hundred yards behind them now. He was shouting repeatedly at them to stop. Missy kept stopping and looking back toward him when he'd yell. Then she would resume her position next to Sammie.

About thirty seconds later, the guard was close enough to fire a shot from his handgun. The round hit a stone between Missy's feet and Sammie's. Startled, Missy jumped away with a yap. She bounded to the left and disappeared into the shrubbery. Bert didn't have time to check on her, he fired one shot back at the guard. Despite the distance, he knew he came close when the man crouched down for a second before resuming his pursuit.

Something primeval was awakened in Missy. Her pack was threatened. As she circled in the woods, out of sight, she was no longer the hunted. She was now an ambush predator. She moved down the slope until she was abeam the threat.

The guard was running almost at full stride. He knew he was gaining on the fleeing group. He was also very clear on his orders. If they attempted to escape, he had authority to shoot to kill, all of them. His eyes moved from path to prey and back to path, picking his way among the occasional stones and limbs. Too late, his peripheral vision saw the ball of hair and teeth coming from his left side.

Missy hit him at full charge, sinking her teeth into his left leg and knocking him off his feet. As he tried to get up, she charged again, this time her fangs headed for his neck and a kill bite. The guard threw up his hands, and as he lost his balance, he fell backward. The canyon wasn't all that deep, but it was deep enough. The first fall was straight over a ten-foot cliff, and then onto a steep rocky roll to the canyon bottom. Missy stood atop the cliff, watching as her assailant came to a stop among a tangled pile of brush and logs. He didn't move. After several seconds, she turned and ran after her pack.

Her alpha male had seen her take out the guard, and he knew that threat was neutralized. However, he also knew that one other guard from the retreat had already crossed the fence and was on their trail. He continued to lead the young couple toward the approaching top of the slope. The other guard would make double their pace, and he would catch them before they could get down the other side. He waited for Andrew and Sammie to catch up to him and pulled out his phone. Finally, he had enough signal to send a quick text to Governor Patterson. Just in case the Governor's phone was being monitored, he also sent a text to Betsy Patterson, for the Governor. With the kids now at his side, he resumed the lead onward. As he trotted, an unsettling thought crept in.

The mystery man and his Husky had been gone for about 45 minutes, nowhere to be seen. Where had they gone? Bert now began to consider that this might be the last resort of the kidnapping plot. What if he was intentionally lured up here to rescue the kids. What if the plan was to kill him on the downside of this low mountain, and then kill the two young people with his handgun, making it look like he shot them? This could be the "plan B" of the entire plot, to try to frame Bert for the whole thing. Was he going over this ridge into the sights of a rifle?

All he could do is exercise vigilance and caution, keeping his eyes peeled in every direction while finding the easiest path for Sammie to follow. As they began to cross the top, Bert stopped frequently to look and listen. He knew the second guard had gained significantly on them and was probably less than a hundred yards behind. He didn't remember the top being so rough and strewn with large boulders the size of vehicles. They had apparently come out higher than his original crossing. He had to climb onto one of the big rocks in order to look for the game trail that would take them down to the highway. He motioned for Andrew and Sammie to continue in the best direction. That was a mistake!

While searching for signs of the game trail, Bert suddenly became aware that all three of his companions were out of sight among the boulders and brush. He yelled for them to hold their position and climbed down. Where was that guard? He had to be up here by now, but he was not in view. He heard Andrew call for him from somewhere roughly forty or fifty yards away. Working his way around the big rocks, he cautiously headed in the direction of Andrew's voice. The guard had also heard Andrew, and he was closing in.

Andrew Atkins and Sammie Patterson stood side by side, her hand in his, listening for Bert. Missy was nearby but out of sight, searching among the rocks. The remaining lone security guard appeared from behind the large boulder to their left, his gun trained on them. He ordered them to not move.

Bert heard the order from his position on the other side of a boulder to their right. He yelled to the guard to give it up and drop his weapon.

"Plan C," thought the guard. Without hesitation, he aimed at Sammie and pulled the trigger.

Andrew saw the look in the man's eyes and knew he was going to kill them. He lunged in front of Sammie to push her away and down. This young man who had been the subject of unfounded accusation, manhunt, and often scorn, now threw himself in front of the young woman he thought of like a sister. He gave his life to save her. The bullet struck him squarely in the back, penetrating his heart, lodging against his breastbone, and killing him instantly. As he crumpled in her arms, Sammie was now the lone target.

The guard aimed again at Sammie, but before he could squeeze the trigger, Missy's teeth buried themselves in his wrist. She had raced around the boulder before Bert could get around it and lunged at the assailant. The force of her bite shattered the guard's wrist, but he managed to shift the handgun into his other hand. Before he could level the gun, the force of two bullets from Bert's 40 caliber Ruger struck him in the upper chest and neck. With Missy still clutching his broken arm, he stumbled backwards against the boulder and slumped to the ground.

Recognizing that her attacker was down for good, Missy let him go after a few seconds and ran to first Bert, and then Sammie. She whined excitedly as Bert gathered the crying young woman in his arms and held her tightly. Her emotions were overflowing and only his arms could wrap around her sudden grief. She pushed away and knelt beside the lifeless body of her adopted brother, holding his hand and laying her head on his chest, sobbing uncontrollably.

For several minutes, Bert knelt beside Sammie, resting his hand on her back and stroking her hair, trying to console her. He knew that nothing would, right now. He also knew that the threat wasn't over. They had to get going. There was nothing he could do for Andrew at this moment. If that life was not to be lost in vain, he had to get Sammie to her parents. There was one more assailant, still waiting somewhere in these woods. Somewhere along the game trail, probably, with an animal capable of killing Missy, too. He gently pulled Sammie to her feet, and urged her to go with him, holding her hand tightly. They headed toward the game trail which he had finally located, leaving the man who saved her life lying near the one who had tried to take it.

The hour-long hike back down the trail to the highway was even longer. Bert was cautious and vigilant to the extreme, looking for the grey-haired guy and his dog. Waiting for a bullet, which he felt certain was to come his way. None did. He did not see man nor dog all the way to the highway.

With Missy back on the leash for added safety, he led her and Sammie to the entrance to the retreat, and to Norah. As he approached the pickup, he could tell from Norah's eyes that she knew what happened. He didn't have to explain it to her, and her tears told him it was best to let her grieve silently in her own way. He opened the back, driver's side door of the extended cab, letting first Missy and then Sammie in the back seat. He entered the drivers' seat, started the engine, and turned on the heat. Sammie was shivering by now, probably both from being cold and stressed out. He knew that Sam and Betsy Patterson would be there any minute now. Others too.

Within ten minutes, the Governor's staff car arrived. Sam and Betsy ran to the pickup, and gently tugged their daughter out and hugged and kissed her profusely. Tears of both joy and grief flowed freely, when Bert told them about Andrew. Sobbing through tear-filled eyes, they led their daughter to the staff car. As she entered, other vehicles began to arrive. First was the Atkins.

Jim and Andrea broke down upon the news of their son. After telling Sam, Betsy, and Sammie how glad they were for them, Jim and his wife leaned against the rear of the staff car, hugging and crying in the anguish that only a parent can know.

Just a minute later, Police Chief Holcomb arrived with the fanfare of four patrol cars, all lights flashing. Bert could tell he was very nervous as he tried to look professional in his duties, knowing the state cops would be here soon. He had larger fish to fry, though, because another cop car arrived a minute later. This was a staff car of the Governor's security team. Betsy had gotten Bert's text message.

Sergeant Doug Blanchard exited the car along with three other hand-picked members of the Governor's team. He walked up to the Governor's window, spoke briefly to him, and then pulled his team together. After a brief discussion, they walked as a team over to Chief Brian Holcomb. Doug spoke one sentence: "Chief Holcomb, at the direction of Governor Samuel Patterson, you are under arrest for the kidnapping of Sammie Patterson." Doug took great delight in putting the handcuffs on Holcomb, giving them an extra click for good measure. With another member of his team on the other side, they led Holcomb to their staff car, pushed him into the back seat, and departed for Cheyenne. The Chief was going to get a taste of his own jail.

Bert climbed in the pickup with Norah. He looked at her lovingly, and then told her he needed to talk to the Atkins before they left. He had to tell them how their son died.

As he walked to Jim and Andrea's vehicle, a revelation was coming over him. Something had changed in himself, and he was just now becoming aware of it. He was compelled to talk to them now. "Jim and Andrea, again, I am so sorry for your loss. I know words can never replace your son, but I'm compelled to tell you some things before you leave here. These are things that your son would want you to know."

Jim looked at Bert from his drivers' seat. His eyes were red with tears. He couldn't drive home yet. "Yes, Bert, go ahead. I want to know what you know. We both do." Andrea nodded in agreement.

"Your son was doing everything in his power to protect Sammie, both during captivity and during the escape today. He fought off the guards twice when they attempted to rape her. He protected her like the big brother he considered himself to be. Today, he lost his life in one last effort to save her, and he did save her. She would be dead except for Andrew. I want you to know that. He would want you to know that he was an honorable and loving son right to the end. He would want you to know that even as he crosses over to the spirit world, he loves you and will always love you. He would want you to be proud of the young man you raised."

Jim and Andrea both began to cry, both from their loss but also from Bert's words. "You talk as if you know what he would want to say to us, Bert." Jim looked at him through his tears.

Bert looked his friend in the eyes and replied. "Yes, Jim, I do know what he wanted you to know." Bert looked at Andrew's spirit and nodded. Andrew gave a nod back and turned away. He disappeared.

Bert walked forward to the Governor's car. He told Sam how glad he was at Sammie's safe return.

Sam and Betsy both renewed their heartfelt thanks to Bert. "Bert," Sam said, "As soon as I get back to the Statehouse, I'm going to set the full weight of the law onto this entire scheme. A lot of heads are going to roll before this is done."

"Good," Bert responded, "A bunch of people need to go down over this. Let me know if I can be of any more assistance. I'm going to miss our talks over pie and lunch, though it's going to take a while to get my weight back under control." He laughed.

"Bert, you know that once this full story gets out, your business is going to explode. You're going to need to start hiring, I suspect!"

Bert started to chuckle, but then realized that Sam was serious. He paused to reflect on that. "You may be right, my friend. I think I know a new private investigator back in Cheyenne who might qualify. She may need a high-level endorsement, though, if she's to make the cut."

"I think you can assume the endorsement will be there, my friend. Bert, you may have worked for me here, but I do consider you my friend, first and foremost. Take care, good luck, and drive safely getting back to Cody, Cody." Sam smiled as he motioned for his driver to go home.

"One more thing, Governor," Bert interrupted the departure for a second. The driver stopped. "Boss, I have a suspicion that someone may have planted an explosive device under my Dodge SUV where it remains parked at the motel. Would you mind sending a team there to investigate."

Sam nodded. "Your suspicion is duly noted, and I will call now. Drive carefully going back. The team will be at your car by the time you get there."

As Bert walked away, Governor Patterson called his Chief of Staff and directed him to schedule a meeting for the next morning and summon all department heads. The State of Wyoming was about to do a full-court press on all the layers leading to the head of FamPlan. Criminal charges would be filed by the next night on the head of that organization and as many layers of the onion as they could peel back by then.

Bert returned to the pickup and entered, speaking to Norah as he buckled up. "Honey, there's one more thing that's been nagging at me ever since we turned around on the highway earlier. I want to go back to that driveway."

She looked at him with a smile of understanding. "Yes, I know you need to go there, my Sweetheart; I think I know why. Your gift is expanding, but you didn't realize it until now.

Four minutes later, Bert pulled the pickup into the private driveway on the right side of the highway. As he did, a slender middle-aged woman was walking toward the road from the house. He stopped the truck and rolled down the window. "Hello, ma'am, I'm sorry for intruding, but something made me want to ask how you're doing?"

Her look of greeting changed to one of sorrow. Tears started to well up in her eyes. "I'm heartbroken, sir, if you must know. My dear husband of twenty-six years has been missing now for about ten days. Despite an intense hunt, there has been no trace of him."

Bert recognized the deep pain and despair. "When did you last see him, if I may ask? I hope you aren't offended by my asking about him."

"Sunday, a week ago, he went walking with his favorite companion, and never returned," she said.

"Did the companion go missing with him?" Bert inquired. He already knew the answer.

She slowed her tears enough to answer. "Yes, Nik was his cherished friend, a four-year-old Siberian Husky. They did everything together and were literally inseparable."

He reached out the window and offered his hand. She instinctively knew she could trust this man, and she placed her hand in his. "Ma'am, my name is Bert Lynnes. I'm a private investigator from Cody. A traumatic loss last year has caused me to evolve into a psychic medium. I've been seeing the spirits of your husband and Nik; they've been guiding and protecting me until I could find them. I can tell the authorities where to find their bodies. He looked and nodded toward the game trail and the mountain it traversed. On that Sunday, they happened to see an abduction of a sixteen-year-old girl, and your husband was killed to keep him silent. Nik was killed trying to protect him. They are together in death as in life, and they love you together in death as in life." He handed her his business card, and slowly turned the truck around to leave. He knew she needed time for herself right now.

As he prepared to enter the road for the drive back to Cheyenne, he and Norah simultaneously noted the address on the mailbox. It was the address which caught his subconscious eye when they first turned around here. It pulled him back to 104 Snowy Mountain Scenic Byway.

On the other side of the road, near the game trail, a grey-haired man wearing a leather jacket was standing. A beautiful grey and white Husky stood next to him. They both looked at Bert and Norah as the man mouthed a "thank you" and waved good-bye. He and his beloved animal turned and slowly disappeared up the game trail. They were no longer among the missing.

ABOUT THE AUTHOR

I grew up on a west Nebraska cattle ranch, the oldest of four children. Hills and valleys were my playground; cats, dogs, and a raccoon were my playmates until younger brothers took their places; windmills, BB-guns, and haystacks were among my playthings; horses and cattle were my workmates. Like the hardy people I grew up among, I have many hours working cattle on horses, using heavy machinery, and learning about the flora, fauna, and geography of the region. My early education came by way of one-room country schools. I often rode horses the three-plus miles each way to school or drove myself in a little Jeep. Two-hole outdoor toilets, coal stoves, and kerosene lanterns are among my childhood memories. Because of Nebraska weather, no phones, and no drivers' license, I boarded out most of my first two years of high school. I was athletic, loved sports, and participated in all available sports throughout high school.

Growing up without a neighbor in sight or other kids of my age to play with, I learned to live in my head and developed a vivid imagination. That imagination serves me well in creating fictional mysteries. Work ethic came from being the oldest son and starting to work full-time, outside of school, at the age of eight.

I have a degree in Animal Science from the University of Nebraska, and I've loved nature and animals all my life. Coyotes were part of the ecosystem, though largely unseen. Their howls welcomed most sunsets. The coyote-wolf hybrid was a natural character for this story, and I wanted to introduce it to the reader.

I first learned of the coywolf hybrid from an Animal Planet documentary, "Meet the Coywolf." I felt I knew coyotes well and had almost no fear of them, only respect. Then, I happened to see another documentary named "Killed by Coyotes." This caught my interest immediately, because I knew of no adult human deaths by coyotes. However, an aspiring folksinger, Canadian, Taylor Mitchell, aged nineteen, was killed in 2009 in Novia Scotia by coyotes while hiking in a national park.

I feel that wolf DNA may have played a role in this tragic attack. Such behavior is not typical of the coyotes that I know. For this reason, I decided to introduce the coywolf to readers. While my female hybrid is a well-trained and domesticated fictional animal, the real hybrids are a blend of wolf and coyote and reflect the characteristics of both. The real animals are not necessarily pure coyote-wolf but may have varying degrees of DNA, to include dog.

Readers should understand that this hybrid is spreading across the United States as well as Canada, because of its resilient coyote blood. The wolf DNA makes it a larger, more aggressive, pack hunter, and therefore more dangerous than a coyote. The coywolf, like the coyote, can live and thrive in urban environments. It may be living and thriving in your city. With a typical weight of around forty-five pounds, it's large enough to be considered an apex predator.

I'm a retired Air Force officer and pilot, and I have traveled extensively across the United States, lived in three foreign countries, and have flown in about 40 different nations. I owned and operated a bed and breakfast in Cody, Wyoming for five years, during which time I was a freelance writer for the Wyoming Livestock Roundup newspaper. That experience developed my interest and love for writing.

I worked as a private investigator for two years, in Arkansas, conducting surveillance investigations in a variety of locales and situations. That experience is part of the background for the Bert and Norah stories. I've also had a lifelong fascination with psychic phenomenon.

I have published a third book in "The Bert and Norah Mysteries" series. The third book is called "Into the Light."

Read on for a sneak peek at the next book in the Bert and Norah series.

"Into the Light"

Sneak Peek: Into the Light

My third book in the "Bert and Norah Mysteries" series is "Into the Light." "The Nickel Dime Murders" introduces the characters and lays the groundwork for the following books. I like to provide real insights into the area and history within my stories. The following sneak peek will give you a taste.

Into The Light

CHAPTER ONE: THE NEW HIRE

Bert Lynnes knew that Wyoming Governor Sam Patterson had called it correctly. After the last two high profile and highly publicized cases, the requests for help from his company, B & N Investigations, were increasing. By the end of November 2017, Bert felt the pressures of having a successful business. He'd known that he might not be able to keep up with the growing demand and might have to expand his company one day. It was just coming sooner than expected. Bert did the math and was compelled to hire another private investigator. In addition to Norah's continued presence and assistance, they were going to need more help if they were to maintain their reputation for excellence.

Albert, Bert as he was known, leaned back in the chair at the kitchen table of his Cody, Wyoming, log cabin. He rubbed his chin as he stared out the kitchen window into the mountains to the north of his house. Bert loved those grey and brown mountains of this part of Wyoming, just to the west of Cody in the North Fork Valley leading to Yellowstone Park. They were beautiful, rugged, dangerous, and spiritually uplifting, all at the same time. He considered this mountain valley the major steppingstone which led to the designation of Yellowstone as the nation's first national park.

He wondered if his former career as a military officer had really prepared him for the demands and challenges of having his own private investigation business. He could lay down a deadly trail of bullets on an enemy, and lead soldiers into danger, but could he build a successful small business? When those doubts surfaced, he would remember what his paternal grandfather used to say: "It doesn't cost any more to dream big."

Tuesday, January 2nd, 2018, was clear and cold. Bert and Norah looked out their picture window onto the three inches of fresh snow. It had turned the early morning landscape into a brilliant mix of glistening white, broken by the scattered trees and rock facings of the surrounding mountains. The sun was just rising over Cedar Mountain, which rose sharply to the southwest of Cody.

Wyoming's second national monument, designated so by President Taft, now sat nearly abandoned on Cedar Mountain, nearly three-quarters of the way up Spirit Mountain Road. This road left the vicinity of the world-famous Cody Night Rodeo grounds and wound steeply up the mountain until a visitor could arrive at the steep ledge which led to Spirit Mountain Cave. What could have been another national treasure, this 2,000-foot-deep cave with its sparkling crystals was largely sacrificed to the development of Yellowstone Park. This morning, no visitors were there to witness the spectacular sunrise as it crept over the mountain to light up the North Fork Highway to the west. It wrested the valley from the night and brought its majesty to Bert's and Norah's view.

Bert shifted his gaze from the morning spectacle to Norah. They were once again discussing the ongoing emails with Elizabeth Hayden, in Red Lodge, Montana. She was the mother of the seven-year-old girl having some kind of emotional issue. Elizabeth, or Lizzie as she liked to be called, had taken her daughter, Summer Irene, to three different psychiatrists. They each offered different diagnoses, ranging from post-traumatic stress disorder to schizophrenia. Lizzie just didn't buy any of that. She said she couldn't help but believe there was something else behind her daughter's strange behavior. She had studied the B & N website and felt strongly that they might be able to help her child.

Norah agreed with Lizzie. "I'm sensing that Lizzie is right about the psychiatric evaluations. That profession wants a label and a psychosis for every human feeling and action. They're not happy unless they can put you into one of their boxes. The PTSD evaluation might come the closest. It could be that some traumatic event happened to this child that her parents don't know about."

www.ingramcontent.com/pod-product-compliance
Lightning Source LLC
Chambersburg PA
CBHW032142170626
46808CB00006B/2339